PRAISE FOR

"Fall in love all over again. With ...
Shiri Appleby, Act...

"A subtly addicting, fun, and fast-paced story about the realty of twenty-something dating in NYC."
Courtney Hamilton, Author, Almost Royalty

"A fast-paced, roller-coaster ride through the giddy peaks and Death Valleys of dating in your twenties in the big city, looking for love, and finding yourself."
Phoebe Fox, Author, The Break-Up Doctor

"For any woman who has ever chased love only to find themselves...this book is for you."
Mandy Hale, Creator & Author, The Single Woman

"...Knapp's book combines love and life in a beautiful twist within the borders of one of the loudest, craziest cities in the world, New York City. But what's most interesting is how the characters find solace in the noise, find happiness in the chaos, and find love in the unique."
Kate Avino, The Huffington Post and CEO of Her Culture magazine

"What Happens To Men When They Move To Manhattan? is a fun and enjoyable read about a young woman in search of her happily ever after. Take it to the beach or snuggle up in bed and dig in."
Emily Liebert, Award-winning Author, You Knew Me When and When We Fall

JILL KNAPP

I'm a native New Yorker who now lives in North Carolina with my two amazing dogs. I was actually inspired to start writing novels from watching television of all things. There were these amazing shows I watched growing up and I thought if I could just create a story that touched people the way that these stories have touched me, I would accomplish my goal.

Apart from my novels, I have been published in magazines, newspapers, and other websites including The Huffington Post and HelloGiggles. I am also the Features Editor for the online magazine HomeMade Bride.

In addition to writing, I hold an M.A in Psychology and taught at the college level for three years.

You can follow me on Twitter @JL Knapp.

For my mom

Chapter 1

Amalia

I could tell by the look on her face that she was expecting something from me. She was expecting something to be different. For me to be, in some way, changed.

I'm Amalia Hastings, and on August 20th at 9:17 pm, I was home.

Home. The word seemed funny to me because I didn't have a home to go back to. I moved out of my apartment right before leaving for Brazil and after my friend-with-benefits, Michael, showed up at my apartment, asking me to stay. I hadn't thought it through properly; I just knew I didn't want to live in that apartment anymore. Before my trip to Brazil I packed up what little stuff I owned and put it in storage for when I returned, assuming I would deal with it then. Well, "then" has become "now". So for tonight I was staying with my best friend Cassandra. Who was currently waving at me.

I knew what she wanted. She wanted stories. Juicy ones that involved hot hookups on the sand. She wanted to see pictures. Pictures of the places I went, the food I ate, and the hot guys I met. She wanted me to run up to her in a sun dress, hair braided and skin tanned, and explain, no, to pontificate, to her how life-changing my trip was. She wanted me to playfully link her arm around mine and gush about how amazing it all was. How I was

2

changed forever. That I had a new appreciation for life, food, and music. She wanted me to tell her that I would never be the same.

But this isn't the movies and I'm not Julia Roberts.

The florescent lights above me flickered, making the airport look dark and ominous. I looked down at my hand as I pulled my rolling suitcase across the sticky, tiled floor. Not even my hand had acquired a tan. Three months in the Brazilian sun and my skin remained as pale as ever.

Cassandra was looking right at me with wide, unblinking eyes. I walked a little slower.

For some reason I couldn't pinpoint, coming off the plane felt like a surreal experience to me. Although I was relieved to have landed, and I wouldn't have wanted to stay in Brazil any longer, I still wasn't utterly happy with being back. I wondered if it merely had to do with the fact that I had no apartment to go back to and was feeling pretty untethered from not having a proper home.

There's an old saying. I'm not really sure where it's from or who said it first. Kind of the proverb equivalent of *The House of the Rising Sun*. It proffers, "Wherever you go, there you are", and up until about one month ago I had no idea what it meant. But now it means everything. It rings in my ears like a scolding mother, repeating itself over and over again until I submit.

I finally stood face to face with Cassandra, who was grinning like a fool at this point. She was dressed down for the night, wearing a purple racer-back tank top that showed off her summer glow, jeans, and gold flip-flops. Her blonde hair was pulled into a loose, messy bun and her make-up was minimal, apart from the extra-shiny, coral lip-gloss she was wearing. She reeked of summer.

"Hey," I offered, looking down at my sneakers. I wished I had more energy for her, but after ten hours on a plane it was all I could muster up.

Cassandra cocked her head to the side and smiled. Her hair swung back and forth and she popped her hip out like a model in training. She looked as fierce as ever, even dressed-down in

3

comfortable summer clothes.

"That's all I get? Get over here!" she said, pulling me in for a hug.

I hugged her back for a moment and then pulled away, overcome with exhaustion and jet-lag. I smiled at Cassandra. She smelled like a salty coconut and I realized she had probably come straight from Fire Island, a beach not too far from Long Island and just outside of the city. That explained the dressed-down attire, but not the lip-gloss. Unless, of course, we were going straight back there from JFK airport.

I looked back at the gate. Most people I knew hated airports, but I liked them. They offered a chance to escape. Get on a plane and in six hours from now you could be across the country. You could be in a different town, in a different house, with a different group of people. I think we all took that for granted.

I could go back to Brazil right now. Or I could go somewhere else. I've never been to Cincinnati; I wonder what it's like there. Or maybe Savannah. I could definitely live in Savannah! I took a step backwards, away from Cassie. Back toward the inside of the airport. She just smiled.

"Very funny, Amalia!" she said through perfectly white teeth. "Don't sneak away from me now. I'm so glad you're back, I really missed you."

Cassie threw her arm over me and smushed our faces together. She whipped out her iPhone and flipped the camera application around so the front lens could be used and snapped a picture of the two of us. Before I knew it, she uploaded the picture to Facebook with the caption "So excited, Amalia is officially home!"

Without glancing back, she walked a few feet in front of me and remained glued to her phone. The back of her Havaianas smacking onto her heels echoed throughout the now nearly empty hallway. I let out a long sigh that Cassandra didn't hear and pulled my suitcase toward the exit. Yep, it was official. I was home.

4

Chapter 2

Olivia

"Would you like a glass of wine?" Alex asked me, as he glided over to the liquor cabinet.

"Red, please," I craned my neck to answer.

I was quite cozy on the couch. The last week of summer had come and gone in a blur of tapas restaurants and strolls in Central Park. Monday marked the first day of our second year in graduate school and I couldn't wait for it to begin. Ask most people and they'll tell you summer is their favorite month. Not me, I'm partial to autumn. Summer is too crowded here in Brooklyn. The restaurants open their side entrances to create manufactured, outdoor seating areas so New Yorkers can pretend like they're enjoying a nice day outside. I've often heard people say that the city clears out on the weekends during the summer months. But I have yet to see this happen.

Frankly, I'm a little sick of it.

During the summer months, everyone is in "vacation mode". Vacation mode for girls means they'll actually go a day without flat-ironing their hair, and for guys it means they'll just hookup more than usual.

Autumn is different. Autumn is the time of the year that signals a new start for me. I always remember my mom putting me in my knee-length red dress and tucking my long brown hair behind my ears while scooting me off to school with a kiss on the forehead. Every first day of school, she would take a picture of me flaunting my new lunch box. For first grade it was "Where In The World Is Carmen Sandiego?"

Now that I am an adult and no longer living in Rhode Island, I look forward to autumn even more. I do this essentially because I want everyone's "vacation mode" to end, and for everything else to just go back to normal.

Alex slipped in beside me, put the wine glasses down, and put his arm around my shoulders. I immediately let my head drop to the side to rest onto him. I was really into Alex. His deep, soulful eyes still sent as many shivers down my spine as the day we met. Next week would mark a year since we'd been together, and we had already made dinner reservations at some restaurant on Roosevelt Island that I had never heard of. Sandwiched in between Manhattan and Queens, Roosevelt Island was a small area in New York City. There isn't a ton of nightlife there, but the housing is more affordable than Manhattan, and most apartments offer large, sweeping views of the Manhattan sky-line. It was mainly inhabited by young families. I didn't really understand why he wanted to live there, but I guess there are worse places. Like the Bronx.

"Last weekend before school starts back up, baby," he said. He raised his right hand and smoothed down his hair. "Are you ready to do it all again?"

"Just one more year after this, and then it will all be over," I said, reaching for my wine.

The fact that we still had two years left in school was wearing on me now more than ever. Alex and I were in a good place, but I worried about what all the stress of schoolwork was going to do to our relationship. At first it seemed perfect, we had something crucial in common. But I started to question if the pressure of finishing school and beginning our careers would be too much for our relationship to handle.

"Have you spoken to Amalia yet?" he asked, now running his fingers through my hair.

"No, I haven't heard from her in a few weeks, actually. Why?"

"I just saw on Facebook that she's back," he said, through a smirk.

I had forgotten that Amalia was coming home tonight.

"That's right, today is the 20th." I rubbed my forehead and let out a long, drawn-out sigh.

Alex rolled his eyes and leaned back into the couch.

"Why don't you like her?" I asked, with a smile. "She's never done anything to you."

"I'm just kidding around," he uttered.

I shot him a look.

"What? I am!" he added. He cocked his head to the side and raised an eyebrow.

I let out a small laugh. He was too cute to be mad at.

Alex winked at me and took a sip of his wine. Alex and Amalia had always been terse with each other. Now that he and I were in a relationship, I really wanted them to get along. My college boyfriend, Nate, and my old roommate never saw eye to eye, and it made those two years of my life more difficult than needed.

"I'd really appreciate it if you tried a little harder to be friendly toward her," I said, raising my eyebrows. "She's pretty cool, once you get to know her."

Alex took a large gulp of wine and widened his gorgeous eyes. They were my favorite feature about him.

"Okay, Olivia, I'll make you a deal. As long as she doesn't give me a hard time, I will do my best to be her, you know," he turned away.

"Her what?" I goaded, smiling at his discomfort.

"You know. Her friend," he dramatically stuttered over the word "friend".

"That's very noble of you, Alex. I appreciate the gesture." I rolled my eyes.

"It's what I'm here for, my dear," he whispered softly.

He leaned over and brushed a piece of my hair from my face that had fallen out of my ponytail. I looked in his eyes and he kissed me. Softly and slowly. A moment later my blood pressure kicked up a few notches. I playfully pulled away, but then kissed his forehead to show my affection.

"You kiss by the book," I mumbled jokingly.

"And you're adorable," he said with a smile.

I pulled myself out of the daze and redirected our attention back to the topic at hand.

"I wonder what's going to happen with Michael now that she's back," I turned around on the couch and leaned into Alex. His arm immediately wrapped around me as I laid my head on his chest.

"What do you mean?" he asked. He lifted me slightly and gently leant his head on top of mine.

"Well, you know." I took a sip of my wine and returned to using him as a body pillow.

"I'm just wondering if it's going to be awkward between the two of them now that she's back," I offered, stretching to reach in my purse for my cigarettes.

"Why would it be awkward?" he asked, stealing a cigarette from my pack.

He inched up a bit and pulled a green lighter from his back pocket, lighting both of our cigarettes.

I inhaled deeply and let the nicotine rush over me. I had been smoking since college and every year I swore I was going to quit.

"Because they were hooking-up for the better part of last year," I said. "And it's probably going to be a little weird for them now. Honestly, I just don't want to deal with any of the drama. Amalia's my friend, but you should have heard her go on and on about Michael last semester. It was exhausting."

I took another long drag of my cigarette, and ashed into the ceramic tray centered on the coffee table.

"What the hell are you talking about?" he said, now gently

moving me to sit upright. "When were they hooking-up? Wasn't Michael dating that Marge chick last year?"

I hadn't spoken about Amalia and Michael's indiscretion to Alex. I had always assumed he knew, that Michael had at some point told him. But even if Michael had never said anything, he really should have been able to figure it out by now.

"Wow, babe." I muttered, shaking my head. "Just wow."

I guess the cat was now out of the bag.

Chapter 3

Amalia

"I was thinking it would be fun if we could go for brunch Sunday," I said to Cassandra. "We and Olivia should have a girl's day. You know, before school starts back up on Monday. What do you think?"

It was noon on Saturday and I had just woken up. I had spent the night in Cassandra's guest room. After she persuaded me to go out to Fire Island last night, the two of us came back to her place. I caught her while she was heading to the kitchen to make coffee. She was wearing gray sweatpants and an oversized men's T-shirt. Her freshly colored blonde hair was hanging straight to the middle of her back.

Apart from Michael's, Cassie had my favorite apartment in the city. From what I had seen of my friends' homes, at least. She lived downtown, in Chelsea. A convenient five-minute cab ride to most of the NYU buildings. Her apartment building was a walk-up, but she only lived on the third floor, so taking the stairs wasn't too bad. At least not until you were coming home tipsy in three-inch heels. I was currently parked in my pajamas on her white suede couch. Unlike Cassandra, I hadn't drank anything last night. I felt crappy enough from the jet-lag.

"Can I let you know?" she asked, reaching for the kettle. "It's just that I might have a date with this guy Brandon." She wasn't making eye contact and her overall demeanor suggested she was distracted by something. I just chalked it up to her being tired. We were out until very late last night. Cassandra had dragged me out to a bar and wouldn't even think about leaving until last call.

"Brandon? Who is this Brandon? Tell me about him!" I jumped up from the couch and joined Cassie in the kitchen area. It had been all summer since Cassie had regaled me with tales from her dating world, and I was chomping at the bit to hear one.

"What's to tell?" She carefully peeled a banana.

"What's to tell?" I laughed. "How about everything? For starters, how old is he?"

"I think he's thirty-one," she offered, taking the now-whistling kettle off the electric stove top.

"Well, where does he work?" I smiled, trying to encourage Cassandra to dish. "And more importantly, how did you meet?"

"He works in advertising."

I nodded and waved my hands around, gesturing for her to continue. She handed me a mug and motioned for me to sit on one of the counter stools.

"Did you meet at some fabulous work party?" I joked. One of the perks of Cassie's job was that she always had an invite to the opening of one of Manhattan's up-and-coming hot spots. She had been working at the magazine ever since college, and it seemed with each passing year her job became more and more demanding. But at the same time more rewarding.

"I wouldn't exactly say fabulous, but yes. We met at a new bar that just opened on the Lower East Side," she explained, sipping her coffee.

I smiled but felt myself cringe at the same time. The Lower East Side had to be my least- favorite neighborhood in all of Manhattan. It was littered with "up-and-coming" bars and night clubs, which I referred to as "seedy-chic" establishments. I thought back to the Manhattan I knew when I was a kid. I always thought of it as classy and romantic. Like an old black-and-white movie. Or at least that's how everyone pretended it was. I wondered when we traded in our Audrey Hepburn phase for a more dilapidated version of New York.

"Do you like him?" I asked, encouraging Cassie to move the conversation along. "Is he your type?"

She just nodded and smiled.

I waited a few more seconds for her to tell me all of the juicy details, as usual, but she just sat quietly finishing her coffee and banana. I stared at her for a moment and tried to read her facial expression. She was acting unusual. Usually after a date she'd give me a play by play of the night's events, down to the brand of lipstick she had chosen. Instead, she continued to sit quietly until a few seconds later, when her phone buzzed, and she reached for it with her free hand and was soon completely absorbed in the email.

"Hey, Cassie," I stared. "Is everything alright?"

"Of course," she said, collecting the now-empty coffee mugs. The mugs were black; part of a matching set her mother had given her when she first moved into this apartment. Along with coordinating bowls and dishes. She crossed over to me and gave me a weary smile. "Why wouldn't it be?"

I know she was trying to come off as being polite, but the question sounded more like a challenge.

"I'm not sure," I said quietly. I tucked my hair behind my ears and shrugged. "The thing is, I just got back from my trip. And you don't really seem all that happy to see me."

I wasn't sure why, but I felt nervous bringing this up to her. Cassandra and I could usually talk about anything. I couldn't quite put my finger on it, but something about her seemed different.

She rinsed off the mugs and walked back over to the counter top.

"I am happy to see you," she uttered, sounding exasperated. She started fidgeting with her long blonde hair, pulling it in and out of a ponytail. "I am just really stressed out with work, and I'm not even sure what time I am going out on this date on Sunday.

14

I absolutely want to spend time with you, I have just been really busy lately."

"Of course. I understand," I replied, quietly studying her laminate counter top. Her explanation had sounded more like a scolding. I wasn't sure why she was acting this way, but my gut told me something strange was definitely going on.

"Listen, if anything changes I'll let you know," she offered. She wasn't even looking at me now, her attention was completely dominated by her cell phone.

"Sure. No problem," I grimaced.

I waited a few more seconds and then, without Cassie even noticing, I slipped off the counter stool and headed back to her guest room.

Chapter 4

Olivia

I had just gotten off the phone with my dad when I heard a loud, urgent knock on my door. I glanced at the clock, four in the afternoon. I wasn't expecting anyone. When I opened the door, I was shocked to see Amalia. She was standing there with a suitcase and a broken smile. Her curly blonde hair was frizzier than usual, and her blue eyes were wet and red. She had either just been crying or she was coming down with the flu.

"Holy crap! What are you doing here?" I gasped.

She rolled her puffy eyes and placed her suitcase on the floor, all the while still standing in my doorway.

"I'm back!" she said, with faux enthusiasm. "Did you miss me?"

"Yes, I can see that. Well, welcome back!" I pulled her in for a hug. "I thought you were staying with Cassandra!"

"Well, I am. I mean, I was," she mumbled. "I think. I'm not sure anymore." She paused for a moment. "I don't think I want to stay with her."

"What do you mean? Why not?" I motioned for her to come inside. "Did something happen?"

Amalia sat down on my couch and ran her fingers through her hair. I think she noticed how frizzy it was becoming because seconds later she pulled a small mirror from her purse and tried to smooth it out.

"Well, I got there last night and she just seemed so distracted. I mean I understand everyone has their own shit going on, but I had just come home after being gone for three months!" she said, her eyes tearing up. She took a deep breath, steadying herself, and began again. "I wanted to just crash when I landed, but she dragged me out to Fire Island until four in the morning! I have no idea who any of the people were that she was hanging out with. In all seriousness, she flat-out ignored me the whole time we were there. I mean, I just got back to New York and I figured she'd want to spend some time with her best friend, you know?"

I opened my mouth to speak, but she wasn't done yet.

"And then this morning, I'm trying to ask her about this guy she 'might have a date with', and she acts like I'm the C.I.A debriefing her on her latest mission. I don't know what's going on with her, but I don't feel comfortable staying there. I don't feel welcomed."

I shook my head. "I don't understand why she acted that way," I offered, genuinely unsure.

"I don't either. It's like she's changed. Or something," she muttered, shaking her head. Her face was washed with disbelief and anxiety. "Did the two of you hang out at all this summer while I was gone?"

"No. I haven't seen her since that day at your apartment when we all said goodbye to you," I said. Amalia sunk her shoulders. "I'm sorry, I wish I had more to go on."

She looked at the floor and then back up to me. Her eyes started to water-up again, but she shook her head in an effort to compose herself.

"Great to be back," she mumbled with a cracking voice.

"You must be exhausted," I placed my hand lightly on her back. "Do you want some tea?"

"That would be great, thank you."

I walked into the kitchen and turned on the electric kettle, a little gift from Alex. Looking back at Amalia, who was now holding

18

her head in her hands and shaking her head. She had come so far last year, realizing she didn't want to put up with Michael's indecision anymore. Last year was a nightmare for her. She had gotten dumped cold by her boyfriend, Nicholas, only to fall head over heels for Michael. We all knew Michael had a girlfriend who lived in Arizona, but he kept his personal life so private I could see how easily Amalia could have put it in the back of her mind. From my perspective, he strung her along all semester. When he finally decided to break up with his girlfriend, Marge, Amalia was already packed and ready to leave for her trip to Brazil. I was so proud of her for not abandoning her plans. After all her growth and self-discovery, it was hard for me to see her have to deal with Cassandra's selfish personality.

"Where are you going to stay?" I called from the kitchen.

She let out a soft, breathy laugh.

"Well, it looks like I am heading back home to stay with my parents," she called to me. "I haven't even spoken to them since I left, so that should be interesting."

I could see new tears forming in her eyes. Between the crying and her unkempt disposition, she looked like a crazy person.

"It's fine, really," she waved her hand and let out a soft hiccup. "I mean it only takes about 15 minutes by train for me to get to the ferry, and then it's only half an hour on the ferry itself. Followed by another 20 minutes on the subway and then a short 10-minute walk to school." Her hands were starting to shake. I wondered how long it had been since she last ate something. "So you know, if I have class at 8 in the morning, I have to leave my house by about 6:30 just to play it safe. But hey, I've always been a fan of watching the sun rise."

Her eyes were wide and unblinking. She brought her hands up to her face and just left them there, as if she needed to hold her head up to stop it falling off. It was obvious that she was desperately exhausted, probably still jet-lagged.

"Don't be ridiculous," I said, pouring the now-boiled water.

19

"You can stay here for a few days."

"Are you serious?" she said, suddenly perking up. She removed her hands from her face and clapped them together. "I won't be in your way, I promise."

I laughed and handed her my old University of Florida mug that I got at orientation my first day of college.

"I'm completely serious. It's not a big deal at all," I said. "But you might want to avoid any further homelessness by finding an apartment of your own."

I always wondered why Amalia got rid of that fantastic apartment she had in the Village. I assumed it was because of all the bad memories. Or the high cost. Money was something our group very rarely talked about. We all just sat in silent wonder about how the other afforded their apartment.

"I think I'll grab *The Village Voice* while I'm out today and start checking some listings," she offered.

"That's a good idea," I sipped my green tea. "You know what else might be a good idea?"

"What?" she asked.

"A shower."

Chapter 5

Amalia

I slept throughout the night. Hard. A solid eight hours had never felt so good. Bright and early the next morning, I began my quest for the perfect apartment. There was no possible way I could move back in with my parents and survive the school year. Or just survive in general. Being twenty-three and living with your parents isn't something I'd wish on anyone, especially not in New York.

Like anyone shopping around for a new place to call home, I had a few requirements. To begin with, I preferably wanted a one-bedroom. I'd settle for a studio if it was all I could afford, but the one thing I did not want anymore was roommates. Overall, Christina was fine. She was respectful and quiet. Liz, on the other hand, was a terrible roommate. Completely inconsiderate and rude. I felt like it was time to try living on my own. I craved the privacy.

The next requirement was that it be close to school. Anything higher than 40th Street, and I'd have to rush to get to class on time every day. Unfortunately my school was located in Washington Square Park, which was anything but affordable, so living in that neighborhood wasn't an option. And finally, and most importantly, I would not even consider living in any other borough. That meant no Astoria, no Bushwick, and definitely no Long Island City. And don't even think about uttering the words Hoboken, New Jersey, to me. I told Olivia all of these requirements over breakfast in her apartment this morning, to which she scratched her head, pursed her lips, and said, "Good luck with that."

With Olivia's help, I had three viewings lined up this afternoon. Originally it was four, but when the words "up-and-coming neighborhood in Brooklyn" fell out of her mouth, I quickly emailed the real-estate agent to put the kibosh on it. One apartment I was viewing was a studio close to school in the West Village, another was a one-bedroom in Murray Hill, and the third was a studio that was somehow "converted" into a one-bedroom in Hell's Kitchen. The last one in Hell's Kitchen was far from school, but I conceded to a viewing just to make Olivia happy.

After a quick caffeine-fix at Bourbon Coffee on 6th Avenue, we made our way up to 7th Avenue and then walked a few blocks down to check out the first apartment in the Village.

"315," I said, squinting up at the address on the top of the building. "This is it."

It was one of those last truly warm days of summer. In about two weeks, fall would kick in and the city would go back to normal. Gray, windy, and cold. Today, the sun was glaring down on me, reminding me of the strong rays I felt in Brazil.

"How's Aaron doing?" Olivia asked quickly, as if she forgot my brother existed. Aaron and I had gotten much closer last year when his girlfriend broke up with him. He spent some time sleeping on my couch and bonding with my friends. Even though he was a few years younger than me, he was mature enough to hold his own in Manhattan any day of the week.

"He's good," I replied. "Busy with school."

"Yeah," she muttered. "Aren't we all?"

"I miss him, though. Hopefully he comes for a visit soon."

"What about Cassandra?" Olivia asked, holding the door open for me. "Have you spoken to her?"

The bleak, gray apartment building wasn't very tall, maybe about five or six storeys high. I could see as soon as we entered

23

that it was a walk-up.

"Not since I called her to let her know I was staying with you," I said, climbing up the first set of stairs. Each step made a loud, echoing sound throughout the empty stairwell. "And by called her, I mean rambled to her voicemail because she didn't answer the phone. She hasn't actually called me back, either."

"When was this?" Olivia asked, holding onto the banister with each step.

"Last night," I answered. "You had already fallen asleep."

"I'm surprised she hasn't called you back yet," she grimaced as we made our way up the second flight of stairs. "She's still your best friend."

"Believe me, no one's more surprised than I am," I puffed. I took a deep breath and held it in for a second. I stopped short and grabbed the metal railing for balance. "Okay, no more talking until we get to the fourth floor."

Olivia let out a long breath and nodded in agreement. A short eternity later, and one quick realization of just how out of shape I was, we made it to apartment number 427 and knocked on the door. A short, dark-haired guy answered. He was wearing a checkered button-down with the sleeves rolled up, tight jeans, and a pair of Converse sneakers. He rubbed his blood-shot eyes, and reached toward a small table by the front door of his apartment, retrieving a pair of thick, black-rimmed glasses. He looked like someone who was rejected from the line at the Limelight back in 1989.

"Hey," was all he managed to spit out. He peeked his head out past the threshold and darted his eyes around the poorly lit hallway.

I turned to Olivia and raised my eyebrows, but she remained cool and composed.

"Hi, I'm Olivia Davis," she said, politely extending her right hand and gave the guy a warm smile.

The guy turned his attention back to us, but stared at her blankly.

"We spoke on the phone about renting the apartment," she continued, sounding a little more annoyed.

"Oh right!" he said, suddenly coming to life. "I'm Eddie, uh, come on in."

We walked into the dim apartment and were immediately hit with thick, blanketed air. I turned to Olivia and made a fanning motion with my hand in front of my nose.

"Did we interrupt something?" I asked, my eyes darting to a half-smoked joint burning in the ashtray.

"Oh shit," he sprung over to the coffee table. "I must have forgotten to put that out. I'm sorry, I thought you were coming over at 4 o'clock."

"It is 4 o'clock," Olivia answered softly.

There was a brief moment of silence. Eddie laughed nervously and walked over to the window, struggling with it until it opened. It made a shrill sound as it slid up, and Olivia and I both winced. I made eye contact with Olivia, who was now shaking her head. The apartment was very small, about the size of my childhood bedroom. The floors looked like fake hardwood and were actually starting to peel up in some corners. The walls were painted gray, but had more than a few white spackle marks covering some decent-sized holes. The fake granite-looking counter top had a red stain on it, which appeared to be permanent, and the refrigerator had a moderately sized dent in the middle. There was no couch, just an old futon, which appeared to function as both a sitting and bedroom area. The only thing missing was a swinging bare light bulb and a rotting corpse in the corner.

"Do you know how much the landlord wants for this apartment?" I mumbled in a near whisper, silently wishing we were in the wrong building.

"Um, actually the payment won't be going through the landlord," Eddie said, brushing some moldy potato-chip crumbs off the brown futon. "I'd be handling it on my end."

"What do you mean?" Olivia asked, suspicion in her voice. "Why would you be handling the payment instead of the landlord?"

"Well, I'm not moving out for good," he took a seat on the

25

futon. I scrunched my face as I wondered how anyone could sit on something so foul. "I'm going to be subletting the apartment. You know, while I'm on the road with my band."

"Okay, then. Does your landlord know about this?" I asked, "And how much would *you* be charging?"

"The rent's $2,000 a month," he said nonchalantly, as if he was rattling off the price of a cup of coffee.

"Right," I nodded, waiting for Olivia to smile. I let out a low, breathy laugh and repeated him. "2,000 dollars a month."

I looked at this guy, expecting him to burst out laughing and tell me it was a joke.

"Also, the landlord doesn't technically know I'd be subletting it to you," he continued. "So you'd have to be really quiet and stuff. Like, you definitely couldn't have a dog."

I put both of my hands in the air and shook my head.

"You're not kidding about the price?" I asked, trying to keep my voice from shaking.

Eddie just shook his head and twisted his face into a look of pity. I was getting pity from the guy who lived *here*.

"Okay wait a minute, let me get this straight," I moved a little closer to him, stepping over a pile of comic books. "You want me to pay $2,000 dollars a month, to illegally sublet your 300-square-foot, potato-chip-encrusted stoner pad?"

"Yeah," he said in a flat tone. "This is New York. That's what apartments go for."

I turned to Olivia, who had already slid into the hallway. I kept up my right hand to the guy, who was now silently judging me.

"No thank you, Eddie," I said, backing away toward the door. "I'd rather live in Weehawken."

"Suit yourself," he said, closing the door behind us. As soon as I heard the lock turn, loud music started playing from his apartment. I could feel the hallway floor vibrating from the base. This was not a safe building.

I let out a loud grunt and dramatically pointed toward the

staircase. Olivia gave me a shy smile and patted me on the back.

"Lucky number 2?" she said, her face turning red from holding back laughter.

I just glared at her and shook my head. I was unable to speak, too stunned by the experience.

"Come on, Amalia, say something!" she threw her arms in the air, but quickly lost her balance and reached back for the bannister.

"Ugh, this is New York," I mocked, in a deep pseudo-masculine voice. "That's what things cost."

"I know, he's ridiculous!" she said. "That's about what I pay for my apartment in Brooklyn, and mine's almost twice the size of that!"

"That apartment smelled like old Chinese food and blood," I declared, making my way down the first flight of stairs.

"Don't forget weed," Olivia added.

"Ugh! I couldn't if I tried," I cringed. "I feel physically dirty after being in that place. Also, I definitely need a drink."

Olivia let out a laugh and sighed. Her brown hair bounced as we made our way down the stairs.

"When I was first-apartment hunting, I almost moved into this place up on East 103rd street that I swear had a meth lab in it. So it could be worse!" she said, carefully descending the staircase. "Besides, you can't really smell blood. It doesn't have a smell."

"I can smell it," I said, emphatically. "And someone was definitely murdered in that building." I pointed back up the stairs.

"You're a liar," she laughed, as we reached the bottom level of the building. "You can't smell it."

"There are two types of people in this world, Olivia," I started, as I held the door to the outside world open for her. The light flooded over us as we made our way outside, and I suddenly felt grateful for the sun. "Those who can smell blood and those who can't."

Chapter 6

Olivia

The Village is my favorite area in Manhattan. Cute little boutiques and coffee houses, random cobble-stone streets, and not to mention the high-end shopping on Bleeker. You also see more dogs being walked around there than any other neighborhood. So when Amalia's first apartment viewing didn't go very well, I was still secretly enjoying my day. I tried to lift her spirits by taking her to Bosie's Tea Parlor on Morton Street.

"I know it was disgusting, but I promise the next one will be better!" I said confidently as I led her toward the café. After all, it couldn't get much worse.

We were walking fast, zipping through a crowd of young girls in black high-low dresses and chunky platform heels. A super-thin red-head then flicked her cigarette on the ground, nearly hitting me by accident.

"Seriously, Olivia, I felt something go through me in that apartment!" she said, dramatically shaking her head back and forth. "How can that guy afford $2,000 a month?"

"I have no idea," I laughed. A couple of cute guys in suits walked past us. One of them smiled at me and I immediately turned red and looked away. Amalia was too irritated to notice them. I redirected my attention back to her and said, "Maybe the landlord doesn't know he lives there either."

"Ugh!" she gasped, jumping in the air and pretending to wipe things off of her clothes. "Okay, I am moving on. How far is this place we're going to?"

"Just about a five-minute walk," I said, taking the lead. "Calm yourself."

I swung my handbag in front of me and dug around for my sunglasses. Realizing I had better savor the last few days of warm weather while I could.

"So, Amalia, you never told me about Brazil," I dug around for my phone too while I was at it. "How was it?"

"Hot," she said, slowing down. "Even hotter than today, if you can believe it."

"Hot?" I raised an eyebrow. "You were gone for nearly three months, and that's all you have to say to me?"

"I'm sorry," she came to a stop. Her eyes darted around the city. "You're right, I'm totally pulling a Cassandra right now."

"Pulling a what?" I asked, dropping the sunglass case back into my bag and reaching for my cigarettes, suddenly feeling a craving coming on. I grabbed her hand to steer her away from oncoming traffic.

"I'm being evasive. You know, like she always is," Amalia shrugged. We crossed over to Bleeker and made our way to Morton Street. "Is there food at this place? I'm starving."

"Yes, there is food," I said, with fake anger. "But seriously, tell me about Brazil. Did you meet any guys?"

"No, that would be too obvious," she said with a tight smile. "Little ole me runs away to Brazil, meets some hot guy named Gabriel, and sets up shop in Rio, only to be heard from by the occasional postcard." She stopped walking again and I took the opportunity to light my cigarette. "Honestly, I spent a lot of time alone, thinking. All of the other time I spent with my cousin who lives there: Julia."

"But you had a good time, right?" I slowly inhaled my cigarette.

30

The smoke rushed through my lungs, and then out again as I slowly let the air leave my body. The craving leaving with a swift wash of relief.

"Yes", she said with a smile. "It was fun. It was a vacation."

"Alright," I said, deciding to back off the subject for now.

"What about you and Alex?" she brightened up. "Are you officially a couple?"

It was the first time she had really said anything about me and Alex dating. I felt a smile tug at the corners of my mouth.

"Yes, officially," I laughed. "There's a certificate being printed as we speak."

"Oh, shut up," she said through a huge grin.

"I'm really happy with him, Amalia." Just thinking about Alex made me feel warm inside. Like Amalia, he and I were hiding our relationship. Unlike Amalia we were both single at the time. We kept it a secret because I was worried about too much involvement from out tight-knit group of friends. As much as it had been fun and sexy sneaking around, it felt refreshing to be able to talk about it freely with my friend. I felt my cheeks flush and I dropped my head down in an effort to hide my blushing. "Let me just finish this cigarette and then we'll go inside. Bosie is right around the corner."

She slowly nodded at me then and turned her gaze toward the ground. Amalia stared at an old piece of gum stuck on the floor for a few seconds and then shook her head. She looked downcast and I worried I had said something wrong. Her blonde curls tousled around her face for a moment until she wiped her eyes, causing her hair to fall behind her ears. I faintly heard her nose sniff, but I couldn't be sure.

"Amalia, are you alright?" I started, but her eyes were no longer on me. Her attention was caught by a young woman walking toward us. She looked sort of familiar, like maybe I had seen her picture before. She had very long, very dark, brown hair. Her skin was alabaster white, and as she got closer I could see she was a few years younger than us, most likely twenty or twenty-one years old. Amalia cocked her head to the side and lowered her eyebrows. I could tell she was searching too. Trying to figure out where she knew this girl from.

"Excuse me?" the girl shouted from halfway down the block. Her brown eyes were narrowed and fixed on Amalia.

"Yes?" Amalia and I both said in unison.

The girl made her way up to us and stood about a foot away from Amalia's face. She was short, about five foot one or so. She wore plain, light-wash jeans and a brown T-shirt. Nothing spectacular. Minimal make-up except for black kohl liner on the inside of her bottom lids. Her pin-straight hair was tucked behind her ears in a child-like way. I noticed she was wearing a gold necklace with a single ruby floating in the middle of her neck. She looked like an average girl. If she hadn't been darting towards us at high speed, we probably wouldn't have noticed her.

Amalia looked at me for help, but I didn't know what to do.

"Do you need directions?" Amalia offered.

The girl ignored her question and looked Amalia up and down. A scowl permanently fixed on her face.

Amalia anxiously started to look around, and then back down at the sidewalk.

"Is your name Amalia?" the girl advanced to her, raising her chin to meet Amalia's gaze.

"Yes?" Amalia answered, her voice rising at the end.

"Do you know who I am?" the girl said, not backing down.

"No?" Amalia recoiled, her eyes widening.

Apparently, that was the wrong answer because the next thing I knew the mystery girl pulled back her right arm and slapped Amalia's left cheek. Hard.

"Oh, my God!" I cried. I reached to grab the girl, but Amalia held up her hand to stop me.

Amalia quickly took a step back and grabbed her face. She winced from the pain, but didn't walk away. She just stood still,

32

unnerved.

The girl shook her head and gave Amalia one final stare-down. Her brown eyes were still narrowed, and I wondered if she was going to hit Amalia again. A moment later, she composed herself and quickly walked away. I turned to say something to the mystery girl, but it was too late. She had turned the corner.

"Holy crap, are you alright?" I asked, rushing to Amalia's side. She slowly removed her hand from her face and tested her jaw. She didn't appear to be injured, just stunned.

Amalia brought her hand back up and rubbed her cheek. She swallowed hard, then blinked heavily a few times. She followed it up with a long sigh. I couldn't tell if she was in pain or in shock.

"I think I'm alright," she shook her head and then rolled it around on her shoulders. "That kind of hurt."

"It hurt to watch," I said, linking my arms with hers.

"Olivia, do you have an extra cigarette? I think I might need one."

"What? Why?" I asked, still in disbelief at what happened. "Do you have any idea who that girl was?"

"Because," she started to say, as she began walking again. "I'm pretty sure that girl was Marge."

Chapter 7

Amalia

"Let me get this straight," Cassandra said, in a tone that resembled utter disbelief. "She just walked right up to you and slapped you?"

Later that day, after telling Olivia I was too upset to get tea and macaroons, we went back to her apartment to veg out. Olivia understood when I called the realtor and moved the last two appointments to tomorrow. Feeling the need to vent, I sent Cassie a ton of text messages until she finally called me back. Usually it only took one or two messages to get her full attention, but ever since I got back from Brazil she had been acting distant. I tried to put all of that on the back burner as I regaled her with my story.

"Yes!" I cried into the phone. "I just stood there, shocked." I was pacing around Olivia's bedroom, replaying the events of today over and over again in my head. "I mean, the girl must have figured out Michael was cheating on her with me somehow, hence the slap."

Cassandra let out a deep sigh on the other end and then muttered something in Italian. Cassandra's grandparents had insisted she learn Italian, so ever since we were younger she would spit out Italian phrases from time to time.

"Jesus Christ, what the hell is wrong with this Marge chick?" she said loudly. I winced and held the phone away from my ear for a second. "Who just goes around walking up to people on the

35

streets of New York, slapping them?"

I took a deep breath and collapsed onto Olivia's bed. She was in the living room talking to Alex on the phone, so I took the opportunity for some privacy and ducked into her bedroom.

"Someone who was being cheated on?" I asked rhetorically.

"Yeah," Cassandra agreed. "I guess that's who."

"I mean I totally deserved it," I started. "Even though he was evasive about the details of his and Marge's relationship, I shouldn't have taken that as an open invitation to start something with Michael." Suddenly images of Michael flooded my mind. The scent of sandalwood, the taste of his kiss, the way my heart would race whenever he would run his fingers through my hair. He had always kept his relationship with Marge to himself, to the point that there were times where I wondered if they had broken up. She lived halfway across the country, so at the time it felt easy to justify what we were doing. I finally came to terms with the fact that I was the "other woman" when he didn't come out for our group's New Year's Eve plans, but instead caught a flight to visit Marge. As the memories swirled around in my mind, I felt a flush of emotion that I had locked away for the past few months. I immediately hated myself for it.

"I wouldn't go that far, Amy," she said. I could hear her moving around in her apartment, her high heels clacking against the fake-hardwood floors. "The girl essentially assaulted you on the sidewalk."

"No, I'm fine," I said, suddenly wondering why I was defending this girl. "It didn't hurt that much. Besides, if her relationship with Michael was anything like mine, then he left her more than a little upset. Does it suck that she took it out on me? Sure. But at the same token, if Nicholas had been cheating on me I'd probably want to slap someone too."

I had known Nicholas for years before we started dating. We met at Rutgers University and after we graduated he professed his love for me one evening. Apprehensively, I gave it a chance.

It didn't take long for his admiration to win me over. On my twenty-third birthday, we got into an argument and he stormed out of a surprise party that Cassandra had thrown for me. A few days later he broke up with me, leaving me absolutely destroyed.

"Have you seen him since you've been back?" Cassandra asked.

"Who, Nicholas?" I asked. "Or Michael?"

"Michael."

"No, I haven't. But luckily for me classes start back up tomorrow, so I'm sure I'll see him around," I said, feeling exhausted by the thought of having to begin studying and writing papers again. "We'll most likely have at least one class together. There aren't that many students in our program." I sat up straight in Olivia's bed and noticed a framed picture of her and Alex displayed on her nightstand. From what I could tell, the picture was recent. They both still had a tan and Olivia was wearing a coral-colored maxi dress. Alex had on a white polo shirt and aviator sunglasses. His arm was wrapped around Olivia's waist. Olivia was turned toward Alex and she was laughing. I picked up the frame and smiled, then almost immediately after felt a pang of sadness and put down the frame. "As for Nicholas, I honestly hope I never see him again." After Nick and I tried to get back together months after our break-up, I realized we had both changed and it could never work. The person he had turned into was someone I could never be friends with. Pretentious, arrogant, and self-important.

"What if you saw him out one night?" Cassandra asked, her voice even. "If we were out to dinner at Nobu and he just happened to be seated a few tables away?"

"Then I would ignore him," I said, declaratively. "Or if I really felt uncomfortable, I would leave."

I heard Cassandra open her fridge and pour herself a glass of something. She paused for a few seconds and then loudly swallowed.

"I know he's a jerk, but you'd really just cut someone out of your life like that?" she asked. "The two of you have so much history together, you don't think one day you'd be able to be friends?"

I wasn't sure why, but Cassandra suggesting I should be friends with Nick suddenly made me question her loyalty. Whose side was she on, anyway?

"Whether or not we could be friends one day is not even a thought in my mind," I said, my blood pressure rising at the mention of having to see him again. "He hurt me, Cass. Worse than anyone ever has, at least yet. I don't want to be friends with someone who could treat me like that. The idea of being around him makes me feel sick."

"You won't always feel that way," she offered.

"Hopefully not," I said. "Hopefully I will get to a point when someone mentions him to me I could honestly say I don't give a shit about him one way or another. And don't get me wrong, it's not like I am still pining for the guy. I am completely over him. I'm just not completely over the way he made me feel about myself."

"How did he make you feel?" she asked, the ice cubes in her cup clanking against the glass.

I took a long pause and stared back up at Olivia's ceiling. I could feel myself getting emotional, the tears forming behind my eyes. But the emotion wasn't brought on by losing Nicholas, it was from allowing him to treat me how he did for so long.

"Pathetic," I said, steadying my voice. "He made me feel pathetic. And no one who can make me feel that way deserves to be my friend."

Cassandra went silent for a few seconds. I took the opportunity to quietly let out a few tears. I glanced around Olivia's room. I couldn't help but be thankful for her. In the past year she had become a great friend. I had only ever been in here one other time; the day she, Michael and I were studying for exams. The walls were painted a fresh, light-gray color, and the furniture was dark brown. Not rustic-looking, but definitely antique. There was a framed Dashboard Confessional set list on the dresser, which was dated May 31st, 2009. I assumed it was most likely left over from her emo days in college. The bedspread I had now made a mess out of consisted of an off-white, eye-lit comforter with a burgundy quilt folded at the foot of the bed. The room felt very warm, cozy. Downright comfortable for Brooklyn, at least. The only problem, as with most New York City apartments, was the hideous HVAC wall unit that stuck out of the only window. Adding a certain sterile feeling to the room. Even with the curtains she had carefully hung, an obvious attempt to hide the eyesore, the fact that it was there would mean this room would never really feel like home.

"Amalia? You still there?"

"Yes" I said, suddenly remembering I was still on the phone. "I'm here. Sorry."

"So how's it going over at Olivia's?"

"Actually, earlier today before the slap incident, we started apartment-hunting," I said.

"For the both of you?" she asked.

"No, just for me," I answered quickly. "I never want another roommate again. Not that Olivia would be a bad roommate. I just think it's time for me to get comfortable living alone."

"Did you see anything worth living in?" she asked. I heard her typing on a computer in the background.

"Not today," I said, reliving the hell that was that apartment. "But I have two lined up for tomorrow after class. One in Murray Hill and one in Hell's Kitchen."

"Nice, keep me posted."

"I will", I nodded even though she couldn't see me. The thought of seeing two more apartments didn't exactly fill me with hope, but it was something that I had to get done. "Hey, what happened with that guy Brandon? Did you end up going out?"

"Yeah, we had brunch at Morandi."

"Well?" I said, raising the energy in my voice. "Do you like him? Did you kiss? Cassandra! Where are my details?"

"Yes, I like him." Cassandra let out a soft laugh. "And yes we did kiss."

"Nice!" I opened my mouth to say more, but she quickly cut me off.

"But listen, I have to go," she said suddenly. "I just got an email from my boss and he wants me to take care of something."

I looked at my watch. 8:00 pm.

"Oh okay," I said, not pushing the subject. "But hey, let's talk tomorrow and you can tell me more about your new man!"

"Sure, I'll shoot you a text," she said quickly, more typing in the background. Followed by a soft sigh.

"Okay. Bye Cassie." I let out a sigh after I hung up, and wondered how much longer Cassandra was going to be distant.

I placed the phone down and smoothed over Olivia's bedspread. I reached my arms above my head and let myself feel a small stretch. I was thoroughly exhausted. I rolled onto my side and checked my phone to see if I had any emails. There was one from my brother, Aaron. I hadn't spoken to him since the day I left for Brazil. I sent a postcard when I had the chance, but other than that we had no communication for nearly three months. I really wanted to keep to myself during that trip. It was nice to clear my mind of everything that was happening in New York. I rationalized that I was too tired to read and write back to the email right then and there, so I left it for tomorrow. Aaron and I had gotten closer, but there was still room for improvement. I closed my eyes and let my head sink into Olivia's down-stuffed pillow. I would get up in a minute and make my way over to the couch, but for now it felt nice. My phone began to buzz and I knocked it over on the floor. No more interactions for today. I was done.

I woke up the next morning to harsh sunlight pouring into my eyes, and the painful sensation of an elbow jamming into the middle of my back.

"Ow," I murmured. I lifted my head up and pushed the nest of blonde hair out of my eyes. Olivia was sound asleep next to me, curled up into a ball at the end of the bed. Shit, I forgot to sleep on the couch. I slowly reached over her and grabbed my phone from the nightstand. 7:00 am. Class today was beginning at 9, and I figured now was as good a time as any to start the day.

"Olivia?" I said softly, lightly touching her shoulder. She didn't move. "Hey, we have to wake up now." I shook her gently. It was our first day of the new semester and I was happy we would be walking in together.

Olivia's brown eyes flew open, like when you see a killer regain consciousness in a horror movie. She turned and looked at me, then squinted. She lifted up her head and began scanning the room with her tired eyes. When she was finished, she scrunched up her face and let out a grunt. "Sorry, I didn't know where I was for a second," she uttered through a hoarse voice.

"I'm sorry I fell asleep in your bed last night," I said, suddenly feeling guilty. "I closed my eyes for a second and the next thing I knew it was morning."

"Don't worry about it", she yawned. "What time is it anyway?"

"Seven," I said, and then immediately yawned myself. "We have plenty of time."

Olivia let out another grunt and then threw the covers off her body and on to my face.

"Okay, okay," she mumbled, coming to life. Olivia stood up and did a full-body stretch. She shook her head around, making her brown hair fly back and forth. "I'll put on the coffee and then we can walk over to school."

"Oh, joy", I muttered, dramatically kicking off the blanket.

We made our way into the small kitchen area and I plopped down on a child-sized chair that accompanied a bistro table in the corner of her living room. Or maybe it was her kitchen. They kind of blended into one room. Olivia grabbed the electric kettle and filled it with tap water.

"Don't forget about your apartment viewings later at 4 o'clock," she said, hitting the power button on the kettle.

"I won't", I muttered, followed by another yawn. "Thanks, mom."

"So last night", she started, grabbing two matching mugs from the overhead cabinet. "I actually thought about something you could do for money. You know, for rent and food. All of that good stuff."

I raised an eyebrow. "Do tell."

"When I was on the phone with Alex, he mentioned that the school is offering a few new Work Study programs for students who need help paying for tuition this year. The pay isn't amazing, but you'd get research experience that you could put on your résumé. You'd definitely qualify, considering you have no job and you're basically homeless."

"Who knew my homelessness could help further my academic career?" I said, getting up to grab the skim milk from the fridge. "Did he say how I go about applying for this gig?"

Olivia poured a generous amount of milk into her coffee, leaving any sugar substitutions out of it. "He gave me the name of the professor in charge. It's Dr. Greenfield. I'll text you his email address."

"Dr. Greenfield, eh?" I sipped my coffee. "Never heard of him."

"Apparently he's new. Flown in fresh from Charlotte."

"Well, thank you, Olivia. That's actually really helpful. And, hey, thank Alex for me too."

"You can thank him yourself today in Advanced Social Psychology," she smiled. "Which Dr. Greenfield is teaching and I believe starts in a little over an hour, so we should probably get a move on."

I looked down at my coffee and slowly swirled the spoon around. There was one question that had been plaguing me since I got off the phone with Cassandra last night. Something I had been putting off talking about. Something I was going to find the answer out to soon enough.

"Hey, Olivia?" I asked, my voice cracking slightly. "Do you know

42

if Michael is in this class?"

Chapter 8

Olivia

"Here we go, again," Amalia stood with her arms across her chest and slowly scanned the room.

The old, rustic-looking classroom was packed to the brim with students. They appeared to be scrambling to say hello to each other after only a short three months apart. Everyone was broken up into their respective cliques. There were the hipsters, the wannabe Blair Waldorf's, the Adderall addicts, the annoying people who always began their emails with "I hope this email finds you well!" and the 4.0's, who barely conversed with anyone who couldn't further their academic achievement.

Needless to say, there was a lot of energy in the air.

Amalia clutched her purse close to her chest and kept her blonde head down. Her jaw was tight and her shoulders were slouched. She was wearing silver sandals, skinny jeans, a low-cut light- blue tank top, and a fitted black blazer. She looked half professional, and half Weekend at Bernie's. I noticed her lagging behind and I dragged her down the ramp of the exact same auditorium-sized classroom we had all colonized last year.

"Hey, I think I see Alex," she said, pointing to a small group of people in the front of the classroom.

I craned my neck toward the front of the room and spotted

him. He was wearing the new Burberry polo shirt I had got him as a surprise gift last week. I smiled widely and he caught my eye. Since Amalia had been staying with me the past few days, I barely had an opportunity to see him. Alex patted the guy he was talking to on the back and made his way over to us.

"Hey darlin'." He bent down and kissed me on the forehead. Then on the lips. "You look great today."

"Hey, yourself," I said through a wide grin. I pulled him in for a hug and took the opportunity to breathe deeply through my nose, silently losing myself in a warm embrace of what smelled like cedar wood and rich nutmeg. When it was over, I turned to Amalia, who was currently engaged in an eye roll.

"Hastings, good to see you," Alex said, with as much diplomacy as he could muster.

Amalia smiled tightly. Her red lip-gloss stretched perfectly over her lips.

I gave Amalia my best "be nice" look.

"How are you?" she asked, still smiling.

"I'm great!" he said, "Now don't just stand there, give me a hug."

Amalia's small frame disappeared next to Alex as he pulled her in for an awkward hug. She recoiled slightly, but he didn't let go for a few seconds. I tried not to laugh.

"This class is packed," I said, trying to break the tension. I looked around and spotted my friend Angela. We hit it off last year, but she was someone I had only one class with and I hadn't gotten an opportunity to introduce her to anyone else yet. I noticed she was talking to some guy, but still decided to call her name out from halfway across the room.

"Hey, Angie!" I waved at her and smiled brightly.

She picked her head up and looked around the room for a minute. Realizing it was me calling her, she grabbed the guy she was talking to and made a beeline over to us. As she came closer I could see she was wearing a long, light-pink dress that looked great on her dark skin, her dark-brown hair hung straight down to the middle of her back, and she finished her look off with lots of long gold necklaces and chunky bracelets. The guy walking next to her was wearing suede loafers, dark jeans, and a blue-striped, button-down shirt with the sleeves rolled up. His head was down in a book, most likely getting a head start with the reading for this class. I couldn't tell who she was with; all I could make out was his brown hair.

"Who's that girl?" Amalia asked, craning her neck to get a better look.

"Angela Edwards," I explained. "She was in my Readings in Behavioral Sciences class last year. She's really nice, you'll like her."

I smiled and reached out for Alex's hand. As I did, he pulled me in closer to whisper something in my ear.

"Did you know Angela and Michael have been hanging out?" he whispered.

Before I could answer him, I turned to Amalia, who had realized a few seconds before I did that the guy Angie was walking over with was none other than Michael Rathbourne. Amalia's face froze. Her eyes were slightly widened and her mouth was tightly shut. She looked around the room for a few seconds, as if she was deciding what she should do. After a hard look at the exit doors, she finally settled for taking a small step back and then looking down at her feet.

"Guess that answers your question," she muttered to the floor.

I had no idea what Amalia was going to do next. Sure, last year she had pined for Michael in an annoying and slightly self-destructive way. But to her credit, he did give her an evasive "stay here with me and help me figure things out" offer right before she left for Brazil, which she rightfully turned down. I was proud of her for that one. All I could hope for her was that the time she spent away helped to shed some light on what Michael really was. Selfish.

"Hey, Olivia!" Angie said, pulling me in for a hug. "Do you know my friend, Michael?" Her hazel eyes sparkled.

47

Amalia winced. But only subtly.

"Excuse me? *Your* friend Michael?" Alex said with a grin. "How's it going, man?" He turned to Michael and patted him on the back.

"It's going well, Alex", he said, returning Alex's pat on the back with one of his own. "Yourself?"

"So, I take it by all of the hugging, that you guys know each other?" Angie laughed. She tossed back her long, dark-brown hair and smiled widely, flashing her perfectly straight teeth.

"We all had classes together last year," Amalia finally spoke. Michael looked straight at Amalia, but her eyes were fixed on Angela. "What did you say your name was? Andrea?"

"Angela," she said warmly, unaware of Amalia's little dig at her by pretending to forget her name. "But you can just call me Angie." She stuck out her right hand and waited for Amalia to return the gesture.

"I'm Amalia," she said through a tight jaw. Her expression was completely empty. She shook hands with Angela and then returned her arms to their guarded position.

"So, Amalia," Michael started. "How've you been?" He bent down a bit to fix his eyes on Amalia's face. It felt like an intimate exchange, but she appeared indifferent to his warm welcome.

Alex and I exchanged a quick glance and he lightly squeezed my hand. I had to admit, watching them interact kind of made me wish I had a bowl of popcorn in front of me.

Amalia smiled and stood up a little straighter. She held her blonde curls up like a crown on top of her head. "Me? I'm great."

For a moment, the five of us just stood there, exchanging silent glances. Amalia caught my eye and offered her a small shrug. I noticed most of the students had found seats by this point and that we were on display for the whole room to watch. I made a mental note to ask Alex what he thought was going on in Michael's head when we went out to dinner later.

"Well, anyway, we should all definitely get drinks sometime after class," Angela said, breaking the silence. "Amalia, do you like tequila?"

Amalia raised an eyebrow just as a loud, masculine, southern-style voice boomed through the old transistor-sounding speakers.

"Excuse me, you five in the front of the room?" His voice was smooth and commanding, the sound of it made me shudder. I caught eyes with Amalia, who also appeared nervous. "Please do be so kind as to find your seats. Now."

He was older than most of our other professors had been. He had to be in his early sixties. He was wearing a navy-blue-colored suit, unusually over-dressed for the faculty at NYU. Most just put on nice pants and a button-down. His brown hair was thinning more than a little, but he still held his head up with an intimidating air of confidence.

I reached for Alex's hand and led him to a row of empty seats in the back of the classroom. Amalia, Michael, and Angela numbly followed.

"Who is that?" Michael whispered to us. "I thought Dr. Browning was teaching Social Psych."

"Me too," Angela whispered back.

One by one we fell into position in the furthest row back, with Alex to my right and Michael to my left. Leaving Amalia sandwiched in between him and Angela.

"Most of you probably haven't heard yet, but I will be taking over this class for Dr. Browning," the professor said, slamming a large, over-stuffed briefcase on the shaky wooden lectern. "He quit last week, just before the syllabi were due. The man is more useless than a screen door on a submarine."

Alex and I just looked at each other and then slowly reached for our laptops.

"So, there you have it. I'm Professor Greenfield and I just moved to this godforsaken city a few weeks ago. I spent the last twenty years teaching and doing research at UNC-Charlotte, and now it looks like I am here for good."

I glanced over at Michael, who was nervously fiddling with a pen. It wasn't like him to show any signs of vulnerability. It wasn't clear if it was the professor or Amalia's return who was making him nervous.

"That's Dr. Greenfield? The professor you were talking about this morning?" Amalia whispered to me. As soon as she did, the professor shot up and directed his attention to our back row.

"Excuse me, miss?" Dr. Greenfield's southern drawl landing on the word *miss*. "Do you have a question?"

"Actually, I do," Amalia said, shocking us all. Maybe Brazil had done wonders for her self-esteem.

"Well then, stand up so I can hear you," Greenfield challenged.

Amalia and I exchanged glances. Alex kept his head down and Angela pretended to be engrossed with whatever she was writing in her notebook.

"Go ahead, you'll be fine," Michael whispered to her.

"I am fine," she shot back.

She stood up, and I half expected her to pull a microphone out of her purse. But instead she stood there immobile as over fifty pairs of eyes turned around in their seats to watch her. Finally, she swallowed hard enough for us to hear and spoke.

"I heard you were running a work-study program and that you are looking for research assistants. Is that true?"

The entire room spun back around, eager to hear the professor's response. Dr. Greenfield just smiled, the kind of smile where you can't really tell if the person is happy or has just figured out a marvelous way to spend the next few months torturing you. He pulled out his chair, which made a scratching sound as it dragged across the old hardwood floors, and slowly lowered himself down.

"*You* want to be part of my research team?" he smirked.

"I do," Amalia said, unwavering. "I think it's a great opportunity."

I heard a few students whispering to themselves. I couldn't really make out what anyone was saying. Just a few select words like *stipend*, *difficult*, and *competitive*.

"Well, then, you can email me tonight and we can set up a

time for you to be interviewed," he said calmly, sitting back down in his chair. "That goes for all of you. Anyone who thinks they have what it takes to work with me for the next year or two can email me after class and schedule an interview. The program will begin next semester, and if you are accepted you will have to take the second half of this course. Which is also taught by me." He cracked his knuckles and gave us all a nod. "Oh, and I'm only picking three of you."

Amalia sunk back down in her chair. Alex gave my hand a little squeeze and whispered in my ear, "You should set up an interview."

I whispered back, "Maybe I will."

"One more thing," Dr. Greenfield added, standing back up again. "This research position will be paid through work study, which means you have to treat this as a job. The last research assistant I had didn't treat it that way. He was slower than molasses going uphill in January, so I fired him. Don't make me fire you. It also means you need to first find out if you even qualify for work study. Don't schedule an interview until you find out whether or not you qualify."

I made out about every other word of Dr. Greenfield's speech, then turned to Amalia and whispered, "We'll sign up together."

She didn't say a word. She just sat in silence and nodded over and over again.

"Now if y'all don't mind, I'd like to start my class," Greenfield said, pulling out a large textbook from his briefcase. "Welcome to your second year of graduate school. Only one more year to go. Let's hope you all make it. As I've already said, I'm Dr. Greenfield and this is Advanced Social Psychology. This class will begin promptly every Monday morning at 9 am and it will end at 11. It will not be easy. The word Social does not automatically imply that we will be watching *Girl, Interrupted* and then writing an eight-page paper on how it made us feel. You will work hard, and your work will be handed in on time. If you can't do this then by all means, please leave."

No one dared move.

"Alright, then," he said, turning on the projector. "Let's get started."

Two hours and four "y'all's" later, Social Psych. had come to an end, and I never felt like I needed a cigarette more in my entire life. The five of us numbly made our way to the elevators.

"Wow," Angela ran her manicured fingers through her glossy, dark hair. "That was certainly something."

"Are you going to sign up to schedule an interview with him for his research project?" I asked.

"I would love to," she said. The second she did, Amalia's blue eyes widened. "Unfortunately, I know I don't qualify for work study. I tried to sign up for something last year and my application was declined."

"That sucks," Alex said, pushing the down button next to the elevator.

"Really?" Amalia spun around, facing all four of us. "It sucks that she was rejected for a program because she essentially either makes or has too much money to qualify?" Her voice rising slightly at the end. A few other students nearby pretended not to hear her mini outburst.

Angela lowered her head and Michael put a supportive hand on her shoulder.

Taking a deep breath, Amalia glanced over to me and I passed her a sympathetic glance. Even though she and Michael had never officially dated, it still had to be hard to see him with another girl.

Just as the elevator door open, Amalia rubbed her face and then smoothed over her top.

"I'm sorry, that was rude," she said to Angela. Angela just shrugged and smiled. "It's just that I don't even have a place to live, so I'm feeling a little on edge right now."

We all piled into the elevator and I hit the button for the ground floor.

"What do you mean you don't have a place to live?" Michael asked, his hand no longer on Angela's shoulder.

"I mean, I got rid of my apartment when I left for Brazil a few months ago, remember?" she explained. "I couldn't afford it anyway."

"So where are you staying?" he asked, turning his body toward hers.

Amalia let out a small laugh and started nervously fiddling with her hair.

"First I was staying with Cassandra, but I got the distinct feeling she didn't want me there, so now I am staying with Olivia," she pointed at me.

"It's true," I said, putting my hand on her shoulder. "We're roomies for the time being."

The elevator dinged once more and we all exited on the ground floor, making our way out into the blinding sun.

"I take it the apartment-hunting didn't go too well, then?" Alex asked, sympathetically.

"No," Amalia and I said in unison. I got a flash of that terrible apartment, followed by a flash of Amalia getting slapped. I wondered if she was going to tell Michael about her run-in with his ex.

"I have more viewings booked for today at 4," she said, with a hopeful smile.

"I could come with you if you'd like," Michael offered.

Amalia sighed and then shook her head. Her wild curls bounced back and forth across her face. "It's fine, really," she said, waving a hand for emphasis. "Olivia's keeping me company while I look."

Michael had a slightly defeated look on his face. I glanced over at Angela, who had clearly noticed it too. I reached into my purse and grabbed my pack of Marlboro Lights, offering Alex one in the process.

"Ugh, just quit smoking already," Amalia said, twisting her lips into a purse. She reached into her bag and started playing with

53

her phone.

"Whatever you say, *Amy*," I smiled, making fun of Cassandra's ridiculous nickname for her.

"Hey, listen, I have to take off," Alex said, looking at his watch and ignoring Amalia's comment. "I have Principles of Biostatistics in 15 minutes."

"I don't even know what that is," Angela laughed. I couldn't tell if she was playing dumb for Michael's benefit, or if maybe this program wasn't for her.

"They just added it to the curriculum," Alex explained. "I'm auditing it."

"Sounds pretty interesting," Michael moved closer to Alex. "Mind if I pick your brain?"

"Yeah, why don't we grab a bite and a drink around 6 at Corner Bistro, and I'll tell you about it," Alex said, looking at me. "As long as you don't mind?"

I smiled and offered him a kiss. His scent pulled me in, and for a moment I forgot we weren't alone.

"Not at all," I murmured. "Plus Amalia and I will probably still be apartment-hunting by then."

"We better not be," she chimed in, without looking up from her phone.

"I should be going too," Angela crossed over to me and gave me a tight squeeze. "I really missed you this summer, we *must* hang out more this year."

"I missed you too," I said, hugging her back. "And we will."

"We should *all* get together more often," she said, now looking directly at Michael.

Michael let out a laugh that sounded more like a cough. His face turned a little red, and he breathed out a short gasp. Composing himself, he nodded at Angela.

"We will," he smiled politely.

"Well, I'm off. It was nice meeting you, Amalia," Angela said softly.

"Yeah, you too." Amalia grimaced and gave a small wave.

Angela turned and walked off into Washington Square Park alone. I threw my finished cigarette on the ground and Alex did the same. He stepped on both of them, making sure they were extinguished. We kissed one more time and I wished him good luck at his next class. He and Michael shook hands and re-confirmed their plans to meet up later that day. The two of them said goodbye to us and walked in separate directions.

A few seconds later, it was just me and Amalia again. I wondered how she was feeling after that class. I couldn't help but feel more than a little awkward. I wanted to ask about it, but I also didn't want to push.

"Want to grab lunch somewhere in Union Square?" I asked, leading the way.

"Sure, I could grab a bite," she linked her arm around mine. "I just hope no one slaps me on the way this time."

"That's a good point. We better not take any back alleys," I said with faux seriousness. "Don't worry, I'll protect you."

She couldn't help but laugh.

"Oh yeah, all five foot four of you."

"Whatever, I took kickboxing over the summer while you were off gallivanting in South America," I defended.

"Cardio Kick Boxing does not count as martial arts," she replied. "What are you going to do? Double-time him to death with your tiny fists?"

"I kind of hate you," I shook my head.

Amalia burst out laughing. Her cheeks turned bright red and a tiny stream of tears ran down her face. I couldn't help but laugh myself. Just then she jumped and reached into her purse. She pulled out her cell phone. It vibrated loudly, but I couldn't see the caller name on the screen.

"Who is it?" I asked.

Amalia scrunched up her face and then wiped away the tears of laughter that were in her eyes. She looked at the phone again, this time studying it, as if she couldn't figure out how to work the damn thing.

"Earth to Amalia!" I said. "Who's calling you?"

She squinted once more and shook her head. Her eyes drifted off the screen and up to me and I noticed a smile pull at the side of her lips.

"Olivia," she said through a side smile. "It's Hayden."

Chapter 9

Amalia

"So, just so we're clear," Hayden put down his beer and rubbed his eyes. "I haven't seen or heard from you in God knows how long because you moved out of your apartment in the West Village, spent three months in Brazil, and now since you've been back your best friend Cassandra made you feel so uncomfortable you had to move out of her place, and now you're rooming with your friend Olive?

"Olivia," I corrected him, while motioning the bartender over for another round. "And it's just a temporary living situation. "In fact, I went apartment-hunting this afternoon."

"Seriously?" he said with wide eyes. "You don't waste any time."

"I have to get back to feeling normal," I defended. "I need my own space. My life is a mess right now and I can't have any more eccentric roommates to add to the mix."

"I agree completely," he said with a bright grin, while he ran a hand through his light-brown hair. "What were their names again? Liz and someone?" He flashed his eyes at me, unintentionally reminding me how handsome he was.

"Liz and Christina," I said, fixed on his dynamic smile.

I smiled back, and asked the bartender for another 7 and 7. After class, I answered Hayden's phone call right away. I wasn't sure why, but I knew that talking to him would make me feel better. He seemed so uncomplicated. So light. It was refreshing compared to most of the people I surrounded myself with. Even though I had only endured one class that morning, school was proving itself once again to be the bane of my existence. Running into Michael was hard, but necessary. I couldn't avoid him forever, especially since we were in the same program. I couldn't deny that seeing him brought back a lot of mixed feelings. Being in Brazil really helped keep my mind off of him, but now I would have to see him nearly every day.

I couldn't help but let my mind wander a bit about Angela either. Olivia said she had known her since last year, but I had no recollection of ever meeting or hearing about her. Still, I couldn't deny that she was a good-looking girl. I just wasn't sure if that was my problem anymore.

"So how are you paying for this new apartment?" Hayden asked. "If you don't mind me asking."

"My parents are giving me money," I spat out. "Please don't tell anyone, it's embarrassing."

"I won't," he offered me a smile. "It's ultimately none of my business."

I shook my head. "It's only for a few months. They said they would pay for the first semester, but after that I have to pay it myself," I uttered. "I am applying for this work-study program at school. If I get accepted, it will give me just enough money to pay for rent."

"When does it start?" he asked.

"Not until next semester," I said. "February."

"Sounds like perfect timing," he smiled.

I smiled back. "I really hope I get accepted."

"On a happier note, thanks for agreeing to meet up with me," Hayden crossed his arms. "I honestly thought I might never see you again."

Having just come from work, Hayden was wearing black

trousers and a fitted light-gray, button-down shirt. No tie, but he was still more dressed up for work than any guy I had seen in the past few years. His hair was a little disheveled from when he had done it this morning, and his sleeves were rolled up twice. An international sign of a tough day at the office, but still kind of sexy.

"Oh, come on," I laughed, suddenly feeling flushed. "You thought you would never see me again?"

"I'm serious!" he took another sip of his beer. "I thought you went off the grid."

"Whatever that means," I challenged.

Hayden looked at me and smiled. He tore a tiny piece of paper off his beer bottle and took another sip. It felt good to have a guy in my life that I could just be friends with. We met last year in a bar after Cassandra and her boyfriend at the time, Bryce, tried to set us up. I was too heartbroken over Nicholas and too engrossed with Michael to even think about dating someone new. Hayden forged his way into the friend-zone, and I was glad he had.

"Alright, fine, I'm being dramatic," he said with an eye roll. "Tell me about the apartment- hunt."

I coughed up a little of my drink and then burst out laughing. I immediately thought back to the walk-up from hell. Complete with illegal sublets and illegal activity.

"Trust me, there's nothing great out there."

"So that's it?" he sounded surprised. "You're couch-bound for the next two years?"

"Well, I didn't say that," I responded, catching my breath. "I saw a few more places this afternoon and while the first two were directly extracted from hell, the last place I saw was passable."

"Passable?" he raised an eyebrow.

I let out a sigh and took another sip of my drink.

"Yes, passable," I waved my hand around for emphasis. "For one, it doesn't smell like weed. There are no creepy landlords, from what I've seen, and I can afford it. Tomorrow I am going back to fill out tons of paperwork, but as long as that all goes well, I will officially have a new apartment on September 1st."

"That's really soon!"

"Like you said," I paused to sip my drink. "I don't waste any time."

Even though I tried to come off confident, I wasn't exactly thrilled with my new apartment. Firstly, I had to borrow the security deposit from my parents. I hadn't told Olivia or Cassandra that, and I didn't intend to either. Secondly, it was walk-up in a neighborhood called Murray Hill. I was moving from the West Side over to the East, but at least the area seemed safe enough. The major selling point was that it was a one-bedroom, not a studio. I'd gladly walk up those four flights of stairs every day if it meant I got to sleep in a separate room than I eat in.

"So where is this fantastic new apartment?" Hayden asked. "And when can I come visit?"

"It's right on 3rd Avenue, between 34th and 35th Street," I answering coyly.

Hayden just shot me a look.

"What? Do you want the longitude and latitude coordinates?"

"I think Brazil made you mean, Amalia," Hayden shook his head.

"No. I think New York is making me mean," I paused for a moment and took a sip of my drink. I looked back up at Hayden, who was fiddling with a button on his cuff. "Okay fine! I will text you the address," I laughed. "But only after the lease is officially signed. I don't want to jinx myself and end up living in Weehawken."

"Alright, fair enough. Besides, I wouldn't want you to jinx yourself and have to leave again," he said, smiling shyly. "I missed talking to you."

I looked around the bar. It was some place I already forgot the name of near where Hayden worked in Midtown West. I had never been here before, but it felt comfortable. It was an older, quieter crowd. There was a faint sound of Nora Jones playing in the background. Unlike the usual heavy bass of the latest dub step craze. The booths were wrapped in thick leather instead of the more commonly seen splintering wood, which I hated, because by the end of the night the place always stunk of beer, and if you were wearing tights they were destroyed within an hour. The best part about this bar was there wasn't an NYU graduate student in sight. I felt like I had slipped into my own little world, a different version of New York City that my friends didn't know about. Something private.

"I will try to stay put," I said. "At least until I graduate." The thought of school and Dr. Greenfield flooded back into my mind.

"Which is when, exactly?" Hayden said.

"A thousand eternities," I answered with a shrug. "Or two years. I can't remember."

"It'll go by fast," Hayden offered.

I suddenly realized I hadn't asked Hayden a single question about himself.

"Come to think of it, I actually have no idea where you went to school," I said, suddenly embarrassed for dominating the entire conversation. "Oh and how's Ernst and Young treating you?"

"Well I didn't go to a fancy graduate school, Miss Smarty Pants," he teased. "But I went to the University of Florida for my undergrad. And work is fine. It's the same as it's always been."

"So you hate it?" I laughed.

"No," he chuckled. "I don't hate it. Just thinking it might be time for a change, that's all."

"Did you say you went to the University of Florida?" I asked. "That's where my friend Olivia went. Did you know her? Her last name is Davis."

"No, I don't think so," he said looking thoughtful. "But I am a few years older than you. Is Olivia your age?"

"She is," I answered with a nod.

"And how old is that again, young 'un?" Hayden chuckled. Just as he spoke, his phone started to buzz in his pocket. He plucked it right out, hit the silence key, and tucked it back in.

"I'll have you know that I am turning 24 this year," I said, pretending to be offended.

"Easy, I'm just kidding around," he said backing off. "I'm only 27 myself. It's not that big of an age difference."

"Better be careful with the whole 'joking around thing'," I mocked him, complete with air quotations. "You're beginning to sound a little bit like my favorite person of all time. Bryce." I never thought Bryce was good enough for Cassandra, he was always a shady character, in my opinion. She ultimately ended up breaking things off with him last Valentine's Day, when she caught him with another girl.

Hayden put his hands up, as if to admit defeat.

"Okay, then I will never joke around like that again," he laughed. "I promise." Hayden looked down at his beer and then back up at me and let out a soft chuckle. "Maybe New York is making me mean, too." He grabbed the neck of his beer bottle and took a long sip.

"Are you still friends with that guy?" I asked, hoping the answer was no. "Because I don't know if I could stomach to be around him ever again."

Hayden shook his head and smiled. His teeth were perfectly straight and his smile was warm and friendly. I didn't feel the least bit intimidated by him.

"Bryce is gone," he answered, motioning over to the bartender for the tab. "He was re-located to Irvine, California."

"Gone?" I slammed my hand down on the bar, shaking both of our drinks.

"Gone," he echoed. "His job offered him more money and a bigger office, so he took the bait."

"Seriously? I remember a conversation, less than a year ago, in which Bryce declared he would *never* leave Manhattan," I said, thinking back to the first time I met Hayden. "I just can't believe he's gone," I pretended to wipe away a tear. "Say it ain't so."

"You're very snarky today, Amalia," Hayden said with a straight face.

I put a hand to my chest and pretended to be offended.

"I'm sorry," I said with a fake pout. "I've just been through a lot the past few days." Hell, I'd been through a lot the past year.

"Don't worry about it," he said in a comforting tone. "It will get better."

The bartender walked over with the tab, which was delicately placed inside a leather-bound book.

"Let me get this," I insisted, reaching for my purse.

"That's not going to happen," Hayden replied. Without even looking up, he retrieved his wallet from his back pocket. Once in his hand, he slid his credit card over to the bartender without even inspecting the bill to make sure the amount was accurate.

"Thank you," I said sincerely. "I get the next round."

"Oh?" he said, perking up. "So there's going to be a next round?" Hayden got his card back and stood up to stuff his wallet in his back pocket.

"Definitely," I grabbed my purse off the back off the chair. "How do you feel about two- buck chuck from Trader Joe's? I hear there's some random brand of wine there that does an awesome cabernet-shiraz blend."

Hayden laughed and held the door open for me as we exited the bar. The sun had begun to set and New York had turned into a more tolerable version of itself. At least for me. At night, it still felt the same as it did when I was a child. Filled with hope, excitement, and the right amount of energy that kept you wishing you didn't require sleep. A wave of sadness suddenly flowed over me, but I couldn't figure out why.

"That sounds delicious," he said, breaking me out of my daze.

"Oh it's a true delicacy," I joked. "Are you able to walk home from here?"

Hayden shook his head. He then walked over to the curb and firmly lifted his right arm

"Oh, a cab?" I said, as I combed through my wallet for my

Metro card. "Fancy."

As soon as I reached into my purse, I felt my phone vibrate. I decided to wait until Hayden was in the cab to check it.

"We can split it if you'd like," he offered quickly.

"No, it's fine," I said with a smile. "I have to schlep back to Brooklyn to Olivia's place. Besides, I am very happy with my thoughts and my iPod on the subway."

A cab pulled up and the driver asked Hayden where he was headed before even unlocking the doors.

"45th and Second Avenue," he called out. The cab driver thought for a moment and then unlocked his doors, approving Hayden's destination.

That was when I found out where Hayden lived.

"I'll talk to you soon," he said, pulling me in for a hug. I could smell his cologne. It was sweet but still masculine. Earthy but not overpowering. Whatever it was, I liked it.

I pulled away slowly and smoothed out a wrinkle on my shirt. For a brief moment, he and I made eye contact. I looked down at the sidewalk and backed away from the curb, waving as Hayden ducked into the cab. A few seconds later, the car had driven away.

It was a long way back to Brooklyn and I felt relieved to know that I would be living in Manhattan again soon. I popped in my headphones and began walking down the street, heading toward the nearest subway line. As soon as I hit shuffle on my iPod, the same Nora Jones song filled my ears as in the bar. I smiled and decided to walk a little slower.

Chapter 10

Olivia

"Don't you ever go home?" I teased, as Alex sauntered into my apartment, unannounced, for the fourth time that week.

I was home washing the dishes that Amalia and I had left in the sink that morning when I heard the door knob turn. Without looking up, I knew it was him.

"I do," he said, walking over to me. "But not when the F train isn't running and the only way home is that glorified hang-glider."

I finished up the last dish and snapped off my plastic gloves. It was something my mom ingrained in me, "*If you're going to wash dishes you have to wear gloves!*"

I could still hear her shrieking it in my ear if I listened hard enough.

"The tram is perfectly safe," I said. "Plus, it's kind of fun."

"Not when it's crowded as all hell and I'm stuck next to some screaming child who thinks it's a theme-park ride," he defended. He rubbed his temples and put his feet up on the coffee table.

His bad mood was affecting me more than I would have liked. I loved Alex, seeing him upset immediately made me feel uneasy. I made an over-the-top sad face and asked him what was wrong.

"Nothing, baby," he said, pulling me in for a hug. "I just got off the phone with my father and you know how nuts he makes me."

Alex's dad was the type of guy who you could never please. If you came home from school with a perfect test score, he'd ask why you didn't offer to do extra credit. If you wrote him a song, he'd ask why you didn't write him an opus. And, most importantly, if you got into an Ivy League medical school and decided not to become a doctor but opt to go to graduate school instead, you would be forever told that you are a huge disappointment and ultimately ruining your life.

I had only met Alex's parents once. Unlike mine, who hated each other and were divorced, his hated each other and remained married. It was like their mutual disappointment in their son joined them together in the fight against happiness. His dad, a cardiologist, worked out of his own practice in Alex's home town in North Carolina. His mom was a college professor at Duke. They were a dynamic duo of condescension and could cut you down with one breath. The first and only time I met them, they came to New York to meet with an old colleague of Alex's father. When the four of us went out to dinner afterwards, they asked me a lot of questions. Mostly about school, but a few about my home life. I explained to them that my parents got divorced when I was thirteen, and I heard his mother make an under-the-breath comment about me coming from a broken home. Seconds later, a quick snicker escaped his father's lips. It was the closest the man had come to a smile all evening.

"He called you?" I asked, trying to hide the surprise in my voice.

Alex's father hardly ever made an effort to contact his only son. Just birthdays and the holidays. The idea of Alex conversing with my father made my stomach turn. It would undoubtedly upset him.

Without a word, Alex just nodded and reached in his pocket for a cigarette.

"What did he want?" I asked, suddenly on guard from the way he was acting.

Alex must have noticed my apprehension because the next thing he did was offer me a hug.

"I'm sorry, I just walked in here in a bad mood," he said in a soothing tone. "He just called me out of nowhere and told me he's going to be in town next week. He wants to get lunch after he meets with a client."

"You never have to be sorry for being in a bad mood," I said sympathetically. "I understand."

Alex pulled out of the embrace and plopped down on the couch. He finally lit his cigarette and took a deep, long drag. As soon as I saw the smoke, I immediately felt the undeniable need to light one myself.

Maybe Amalia was right. Maybe I should quit.

"Lunch, Olivia. I'm not even worth a fucking dinner," Alex's face was growing red.

"So don't go," I blurted out, maybe a little too quickly. "If it makes you that upset, you don't have to see him. You're an adult now. A *busy* adult. And if seeing him is just going to ruin your day, then no one says you have to go through with it."

"Olivia, he's my dad," Alex's smooth expression had twisted into a scowl. "What am I supposed to do, ignore him for the rest of my life?"

"No, of course not," I defended myself. "Not for the rest of your life, but maybe just for right now. Look, school just started back up and we are all on edge. The last thing you need right now is your dad making a guest appearance, forcing you to rethink all of your decisions. Making you question all of your hard work."

Alex took another drag of his cigarette and remained quiet. I was nervous I had gone too far, I had a habit of doing that. Still, I felt like seeing his father was a bad idea. And deep down, I think he knew I was right.

As Alex's silence filled the room, I questioned if I should have said anything at all. I really was no one to give advice on the subject. My dad and I had a great relationship. When my mother and father got a divorce, I lived with my dad most of the time. He and I became our own little team.

Suddenly, I needed fresh air. I walked over to the window and opened it as far as it would move. It made a loud, creaking sound, and the cool wind felt more punishing then refreshing.

"I'll think about it," was all Alex said through a cloud of smoke.

I glanced out the window at the busy city underneath me, loud and chaotic at any time of the day. I wanted to ask it to be quiet, that it was being rude for interrupting us. I sat myself down next to him on the couch and raised my hand to touch his shoulder. He refused to meet my gaze.

"Are you upset with me?" I asked, suddenly worried. Alex and I had never had a fight before. Well, unless you counted that night at the alumni mixer last year. We had gotten into an argument early into our friendship. In retrospect it was about something trivial. So trivial I don't even remember what it was. I overreacted a bit and ran out of the hotel, unable to deal with my growing feelings for him. I felt much more comfortable with him now, and the thought of losing him was heartbreaking.

"Honestly?" he started. He sat up straighter on the couch, and his harsh demeanor made me wince. "Yeah I'm a little upset that you're not being more supportive."

"How am I not being supportive?" I nearly jumped off the couch. "I'm trying to protect you from having what can only be described as a pity lunch with your not-so-present father."

"He's still my dad, Olivia." He folded his arms and shook his head slightly.

Tears began welling up behind my eyes, but I didn't want to let them out. I felt like I was right and didn't want to be told something harsh, like I was using tears to win an argument.

Nervously smoothing out my hair, I tried to appear more confident than I felt. "Fine. Maybe you should go home," I said coldly, unable to prevent the words from leaving my mouth.

I expected him to fight me on it, tell me I was overreacting. But instead all he said was, "Maybe I should."

I snapped my head around to look at him. Before I knew what

was happening Alex put out his cigarette in a nearby ashtray and stood up to leave.

"Wait!" I called, wishing I could take back my request for him to leave. "I didn't mean that."

"Whatever. Its fine," he uttered quickly, and in a flash he was out the door.

I didn't even know why I had told him to leave, and now I was left feeling confused and guilty, with a hint of juvenile. Had we really just had such a petty argument? I stood there for a few seconds in shock. Had I gone too far with Alex? Should I have just kept quiet and let him sulk? Just then the doorknob began to turn. I rushed over to the door, thankful that Alex had come back. Ready to talk about what had just happened.

I flung open the door just as Amalia was turning her key. She jumped back and gasped, her key still in the doorknob.

"What the hell are you doing? What's wrong with you?" she breathed, clutching her chest. "You scared the hell out of me."

Without answering, I looked past her, darting my eyes down the hallway to the left and to the right. Alex had definitely left. I could feel tears welling up behind my eyes.

"I don't know," I muttered, walking away from the door. I didn't want her to see my face, but Amalia followed me over to the couch and, in unison, we both took a seat. "Alex and I just had a huge fight." I gently pressed my palms into my eyes.

"What about?" she said, placing her purse on the table. As soon as she got close to me, I noticed she smelled of alcohol.

"About his dad coming into town and how terrible the guy is in general," I moved my hand to my head and nervously began twirling my hair.

"Alex is terrible?" she asked, cocking her head to the side. She moved closer and put her hand on my knee. "I didn't want to say anything, I mean, he is kind of irritating."

"No, not Alex! His father," I snapped, reaching for yet another cigarette.

"Are you chain-smoking?" she asked, inching away.

"This really isn't the time, Amalia," my eyes burning from fighting back tears. I wanted to ask her if she had been drinking, but I didn't want to come off as more of a bitch than I already had. I also didn't want to have a conversation about my relationship with her if she was drunk.

I lit up another cigarette and crossed back over to the window. I hoped to catch a glimpse of Alex pacing on the street, wrestling with the idea of coming back upstairs. He was nowhere to be seen.

"It's going to be okay, right?" she asked, not moving from the couch. "I mean, you'll see him tomorrow in class."

"No he has that class he's auditing tomorrow." I suddenly realized I wouldn't be able to patch things up with him until he felt like it. Now *I* was pacing.

"I think you may be overreacting a tiny bit," she mumbled, just loud enough for me to hear. She twisted her curly blonde hair up into a tight ponytail and leaned back onto the couch.

"How would you know?" I shot back, suddenly irrationally angry.

"I'm just saying, the two of you seem very happy together," she defended. "I am sure he'll call you later and then you guys can work it out."

"I'm not going to wait for him to realize he's being crazy, I'm going to try calling him," I said, grabbing my cell out of my back pocket. I thought I heard Amalia mumble something about *me* being the one who was crazy, but I may have just imagined that. The phone rang three times before the voicemail picked up. It was clear that Alex did not want to talk to me.

"Damn it!" I tossed the phone on the couch.

"Be careful, you're going to break your phone," Amalia warned. She reached into her purse and pulled out her own cell. She immediately began texting someone.

I threw up my arms and then let them slap the side of my thighs. "Could you do me a favor and leave me alone please?" I snapped.

"Whoa, what's your problem?" Amalia stood up immediately and folded her arms in front of her tiny frame. "I just got here and you're taking this out on me!"

"Exactly!" I practically shouted. "You left for three months and you *just* got back. So please stop acting like you know anything about me and my relationship."

"Well excuse me, Olivia!" Amalia put her hand up. "If I don't know anything about your relationship it's because the two of you kept it a secret from your closest friends for nearly a year. Who knows if you would have even told me about the two of you if Alex hadn't knocked on my apartment door that day looking for you." Amalia grabbed her cell phone off the coffee table and stuffed it into her back pocket. She reached for her purse and gripped it firmly at her side. "And I don't remember getting any emails from *you* when I was in Rio. I'm sorry if I didn't reach out enough, but it's not *my* fault I don't know what is or isn't considered a big fight to you and Alex."

I knew she was right. It was cowardly of me to make Alex promise not to tell anyone about our relationship last semester, and now it was back to bite me. I threw my hands back up in the air and numbly headed to my bedroom door.

"Unbelievable," Amalia muttered under her breath.

Suddenly, I felt really guilty for taking my problems out on her and turned on my heel to face her.

"Hey, I'm sorry," I sighed. "You're right about literally everything you just said. I just feel so on edge this semester for some reason."

Amalia shook her head. She too was refusing to meet my gaze. "I am going to sign that lease soon, so don't worry, I'll be out of your hair."

"No, that's not what I meant," I said. "And that's definitely not what I want. I shouldn't have told you to leave me alone. That's exactly what I said to Alex as soon as he started getting testy with me, and that's why he left. I don't know why, but I feel like I am always pushing people away."

73

"Yeah," she lowered her eyes. "I know what that's like." Something made me wonder if she was referring to Hayden. She tossed her purse and cell phone back on the couch. "Don't worry about it, we'll be crazy together." I laughed and nodded in agreement. "Want me to make some tea? Maybe we could find a terribly cheesy chick flick to watch?"

"Yeah," my shoulders immediately relaxed. "I could really use that."

"Alright," she smiled. As soon as she turned on the television, her phone buzzed for the third time since she had arrived.

"Is that Hayden?" I asked. "Let me get my laptop, I want to google this guy!"

"We're not doing that!" she jumped up and blocked me. Her smile immediately disappeared. "It's not from Hayden. It's Michael."

"Michael Rathbourne?" I whispered.

"No," she put her hand on her hip. "Michael Caine."

I shot her a look. "You and Michael are talking again?" Just as I thought she was finally moving forward with her life, Michael had to swoop back in and mess it up.

Amalia let out a long groan and hung her head backwards. "I did not initiate this. He texted me on the way home from hanging out with Hayden, and he just texted me again right now." She was fidgeting with her cell phone, moving it back and forth from hand to hand. "I haven't even answered him."

"What did he say?" I asked. "Forget the chick flick, your boy drama is way more interesting."

"Very funny," she smirked. "All the first text message said was, "*Hey*" and this one just now says, "*Can you meet up before class tomorrow?*"

"What do you think that means?" I asked, uncomfortably shifting my weight on the couch.

"Who the hell knows with him?" she sounded exasperated. "Our award-winning, multi-published professors wouldn't know what to make of mine and Michael's relationship. I certainly don't. We could analyze this forever, people still argue about whether or not the moon landing was real! And in all honestly, I meant what I said when I left over the summer. I'm tired of campaigning for his attention."

I pretended we were at an award show and started to do a slow-clap. Amalia laughed and stood up, taking an over-the-top bow.

"So then you like Hayden," I nudged. "I knew it."

"Right now, let's operate under the notion that I don't like anybody," she said sternly. "Last semester kicked my ass. I *have* to focus on school. And getting into that work-study program! So for tonight, let's watch *Something Borrowed* and leave all of this texting nonsense until tomorrow."

"I'm so proud of you," I said, leaning over to give her a side hug.

"Thanks," she smiled. "I'll go make that tea now. You want chamomile, right?"

I nodded and checked my phone again to see if Alex had tried to reach me. Nothing.

I knew Amalia was trying to be strong, but I could still tell that any contact from Michael was hard for her. If she felt for Michael half of what I felt for Alex, I knew it was going to be a long semester for her. I just hoped she was able to keep her promise to herself and not let him suck her back in with his charms.

Amalia's phone buzzed again; she scrunched her face up while reading the text.

"Who is it this time?" I asked. "Nicholas?"

"Don't even joke about that," she said, suddenly serious. "No, it's Cassandra. The magazine she works at is having a party this weekend and apparently you and I are invited."

"Sounds like a blast," I said, trying not to sound too sarcastic.

"I feel like I have to go," she started typing back. "I haven't seen her in a couple of weeks." She reached for the teapot and turned on the sink faucet.

"I'll come with you," I said. "It might be slightly enjoyable. Oh!

You should ask her if Hayden can come too."

Amalia touched her chin and looked deep in thought for a moment. Then she shrugged and flicked on the stove. "I'll think about it."

"Come on," I goaded her. "You know you like him."

"I don't like anyone right now," she laughed. "Remember what I just said? I have to focus on school. You remember school, right? The big building with all of the books in it?"

"You know what happens every time someone says that?" I walked over to the cabinet and reached for the box of chamomile. "That they want to focus on themselves and not be in a relationship?"

"No, Olivia," she laughed, grabbing some honey from the shelf. "What happens?"

"They end up in a relationship," I grinned widely. "Or engaged."

"Great, just shoot me," she shook her head. "Now I'm definitely going to flunk out."

Chapter 11

Amalia

Washington Square Park was practically empty this morning. As soon as I reached the end of 5th Avenue and entered the park under the giant arch, I noticed no one but a few guys hanging out by the fountain. They were all wearing jeans and button-down shirts. Probably still awake from last night, I thought as I passed a bed of flowers on my right. I loved when this area was empty. It was just quaint enough to feel like you weren't in the city as long as a bunch of hipsters weren't smoking cigarettes or skate-boarding while you were trying to relax. I walked toward an empty bench and sat down. The wood felt cool from the shade, and in the morning air you could tell that summer would only be sticking around for a few more days. I pulled my light-blue cardigan out of my over-sized purse, which usually housed my laptop and at least one textbook, and quickly pushed my arms through the sleeves. I had gotten up early this morning and gone for a walk before class started. For some reason I ended up here. Just as I reached for my Kindle, I heard footsteps to my left.

"Amalia?" Michael asked. "Hey, good morning."

I took a deep breath and coughed. I had actually forgotten all about meeting up with him to talk this morning. I hadn't even texted him back, but I should have realized he would have had to cut through the park to get to class. I didn't want to blow him off, but at the same time I wasn't really sure what we had to talk about.

"Hi," I said, uneasily. "How are you?"

"I'm good," he shifted his shoulder bag from one arm to another. "Mind if I sit down?" He pointed to the park bench.

I glanced down at the bench. My bag was currently taking up just enough room for one person. I nodded and moved it to the floor. "Sorry I didn't text you back last night. I am staying with Olivia and she and I were up late talking."

Michael just shook his head and smiled. He put his computer bag next to mine and slid onto the bench. "It's fine, don't worry about it. But I do want to talk to you, if that's okay?"

"Of course," I answered, trying to sound breezy. I suddenly felt very warm and promptly removed my sweater. "What's up?"

"I just hate that we haven't really talked in months," he said. He was slightly hunched over, and his hands were folded in front of him. It was unusual for him. He was usually so stiff. So poised. As the sun made its way into our shaded corner, I could see in his eyes that he was exhausted.

"It's only because I wasn't here," I said quickly, noticing his collection of books pouring out of his bag.

"I know," he nodded, his tired eyes locked on the ground. "You went away."

"It's not like I am avoiding you," I replied, even though I wasn't sure whether that was the truth or not. I certainly hadn't made any effort to see Michael since I had returned. There was a distinct silence that followed as he straightened his posture out and looked me straight in the eyes. I cleared my throat and checked my watch. "We have about fifteen minutes before class starts."

"You're right," he said, breaking eye contact. "Are you applying for the work-study program?"

I nodded and suddenly felt a wave of dread over the possibility of working with Dr. Greenfield next semester. "I know I qualify, I'm completely broke. Plus, I need to do something to set me apart from all of the other students here. Not to mention my résumé's a little thin." I felt my phone buzz in my pocket, but ignored it. My meeting with Michael was awkward enough without the possibility of an impromptu text from Hayden making me more uncomfortable.

"I think it's a great opportunity," he offered. "And from what I've heard, that professor who's running it is extremely influential."

I just nodded and smiled, unsure of what to say.

His attention was suddenly grabbed by a gaggle of undergrads loudly making their way through the park, heading to their classes. He let out a small laugh and shook his head at them. As he rubbed his eyes, I knew what he felt. Envy. They were only a few years younger than us, but their lives were completely different. They were still filled with hope and excitement for school. The possibility of getting into the graduate program of their choice or landing the job of their dreams. I was filled with anxiety and pressure, and even though he would probably never admit it, I think Michael was beginning to feel it also. While our conversations were about research studies and making ends meet, theirs were about fraternity parties and tales of weekend debauchery. I caught eyes with one of the girls in the group. She was wearing an over-sized chunky sweater, tight skinny jeans, and brown knee- high boots. Her long, auburn hair shone as she quickly turned back to her friends and giggled, practically bouncing with energy with her to-go coffee cup from Murray's Bagels in her hand. I closed my eyes and smiled, allowing myself to feel her energy for just a moment. Remembering what it was like to still be free.

Michael turned back to me and inched a little bit closer. Even at a quarter to nine in the morning, he smelled like his signature blend. The memory of past events, only a few months ago now, felt like years, but as soon as he got that close to me my heart picked up the pace and it seemed like only yesterday that I was waking up at his apartment, silently begging the sun to stay down a little longer so we wouldn't have to get up.

"So are you and Angela together?" I blurted out, and then immediately wished I hadn't. "I mean, not that it's any of my business." I crossed my legs, shifting about an inch away from him.

"No. We're not in a relationship," he answered, as if it was absurd to believe otherwise. "What makes you say that?"

"She was kind of all over you the other day in class," I explained. "I just assumed maybe you two were together." I wasn't really sure how to feel about this explanation. I didn't necessarily want to be with Michael at this point, but a part of me really didn't want him to be dating anyone else.

"No," he shook his head. "We hung out a couple of times over the summer. Maybe it meant more to her than it did to me."

Wow, I thought. Classic Michael.

"We should get going," I stood up and reached for my bag. "I really can't afford to be late."

"I hear that," he said, collecting his belongings. "I really missed you, Amalia." As soon as we reached for our bags, his hand brushed against mine. I quickly pulled away and tucked a stray curl behind my ear. I couldn't deny that I missed him too.

"Can I walk you to class?" he asked, seemingly unaffected by our physical contact.

"Sure," I took a step forward and he motioned for me to walk in front of him.

As we silently made our way to class, I felt the all-too-familiar anxiety that came with being in proximity with Michael. My phone buzzed again and my stomach dropped at the possibility that it was Hayden. The more I thought about it, the more I realized just how difficult it was going to be to get through this year unscathed.

Chapter 12

Olivia

"Still no word from Alex?" Amalia whispered to me as we sat in class. As the rest of the students feverishly took notes, most likely only understanding half of what Dr. Greenfield was saying, I was anxiously checking my phone every five minutes. She was sitting in between Michael and myself. I don't think she noticed, but he kept looking over at her, almost studying her. Angela had gotten to class late and wasn't able to sit with us. She was a few rows to the right and kept tossing glances this way any chance she got. I felt guilty that there wasn't a seat available for her by our group, but by the same token I didn't want to feel any tension between her and Amalia while I was worried about Alex and trying to concentrate on class.

"No," I shook my head. I felt an influx of sadness and worry. "I'm kind of scared. He's never not answered any of my calls or texts before."

"Maybe Michael has seen him," she whispered, even lower. Michael heard his name being said and looked up for a second. I just grimaced and sunk a little lower in my chair. "I'm going to go by his apartment later and make sure he's alright."

"Alright everyone," Dr. Greenfield clapped his hands together. "That's all for today. Your first exam is in two weeks."

Amalia's eyes widened and she inhaled sharply.

"Our exam's only in two weeks? I better start studying *tonight*." Amalia stood up, but left her belongings by her chair. "Okay, here I go." She smoothed out a wrinkle on her shirt and made her way to the front of the room.

"Where is she going?" I asked Michael.

He unplugged his computer from a neighboring outlet and watched Amalia make her way down to the front of the room. "I think she's going to talk to the professor about setting up an interview for the work-study program."

"Damn," I said. "I should really do that too."

"What's stopping you?" he asked, wrapping his computer cord up into a neat circle.

The truth was, I just couldn't imagine the added pressure of being a research assistant with a full course load. Amalia had approached Dr. Greenfield and from what I could see, kept her composure the whole time she spoke with him. I wasn't sure I could do the same, being in that position.

"Nothing," I said. "I'll just shoot him an email when I get home. I don't feel like talking to him about it in person."

"Fair enough," he smiled. "I'm taking off. Tell Amalia I said bye."

"You got it," I nodded. I watched him look over to Amalia, but as soon as he exited the row Angela caught his attention and he walked out with her. I wondered if they were going somewhere together. Ultimately, it was none of my business.

A moment later, my cell buzzed in my purse and I almost jumped out of my skin when I saw that it was a text from Alex telling me he was outside the building. Relieved, I made my way out of the classroom and opted to take the stairs instead of waiting in line for the elevator. When I got outside, I saw Alex leaning up against the wall of the building smoking a cigarette. I gingerly made my way over to him.

"Can I bum one?" I said, half-jokingly. Alex looked up and nodded, his eyes were puffy and tired. He looked kind of messy.

His dark-blonde hair was hidden under a baseball cab. He had traded his usual polo or button-down shirt for a plain T. I made a joke about him being incognito and he laughed weakly.

"I just didn't feel like sitting through class today," he said, taking a long drag.

"I never feel like coming to this class, so I completely understand." I leaned against the wall with him and reached for his hand. He either didn't notice or didn't want it, because he didn't reach back.

"I'm sorry I took off like that last night," he threw the cigarette on the floor and stepped on it. "And I'm sorry I didn't answer any of your calls or texts."

"Where did you go?" I asked in a worried tone. I tried to keep my voice from shaking, but I wasn't having the best of luck.

"I walked around for a bit," he replied. "Then I went back to Roosevelt Island and went to a bar."

"By yourself?" I asked. I wanted to go easy on him because I could see he was upset, but the idea of Alex out at a bar alone made my stomach uneasy.

"Yep," he avoided making eye contact with me.

I bit my lip and took a step closer to him. Even unshowered and unshaved, he was still handsome.

"What were you doing in a bar by yourself?" I put some strength into my voice. "And I get that you're sorry, but you had me worried sick about you."

"I wasn't out trying to pick up some girl, if that's what you're worried about," he spat out.

I took a step back and shook my head, shocked by the venomous way he was talking to me.

"Actually, the thought hadn't crossed my mind," I lied. Alex was a hot guy, with his own apartment. There would be girls lining up around the block to make him feel better after a blow-out with his girlfriend. "What I am worried about is you. You don't answer my calls, you're going to bars alone, and now you're skipping class! Is all of this really because your dad's in town?"

"I don't know," he rubbed the back of his neck. "Maybe."

A group of students walked by and snickered at our conversation. I could tell they were undergrads and probably had no idea who we were, but it still bothered me.

"Great now people are involving themselves in our private conversations," I said. "I am just going to go. This is exactly what I didn't want."

"What do you mean?" he asked, finally meeting my gaze. "What don't you want?

I sighed and reached into my bag for a cigarette. I really needed one, and possibly a drink too.

"I didn't want my private life," I pointed at him and then back at myself, "and my school life to affect each other."

"Right, the reason you wanted to keep our relationship a secret," he growled. Alex had a hurt look in eyes, but his vehement behavior kept my sympathy at bay.

"Well maybe I was right," I countered. "Now if you'll excuse me, some of us actually have to attend class today."

Before he could engage me any further, I trudged past him without looking back and flicked my still-lit cigarette into the street. I couldn't believe we had gotten into another argument. I expected him to show up and beg for my forgiveness; I guess that wasn't happening. Through my anger, I saw Angela across the street by the library typing on her phone. I decided her company was better than no company and made a beeline for where she was standing. When I got over to her, she pulled me in for a hug and practically jumped up in the air.

"What's going on?" I asked her. "Why are you so happy?

She stepped out of the hug and flipped her long, brown hair.

"Because I just got invited to some big magazine party this weekend." She clapped her hands together. "And you're never going to guess who I'm bringing as my date!"

Chapter 13

Amalia

"Amy! Glad you made it," Cassandra gave me a quick hug in between reaching for a glass of red wine and waving to one of her co-workers. "I want to introduce you to someone."

Olivia and I arrived at the party only twenty minutes past the invitation time, but the whole place was already in full swing. I recognized no one but eventually found Cassie holding court in the back of the bar. She was surrounded by industry types: super-thin women and the rich, gorgeous men who always followed them wherever they went. Or maybe it was the other way around. While Olivia and I opted for a more casual look of skinny jeans and kitten heels, Cassandra was fully decked out wearing a tight, gold dress, four-inch Jimmy Choo's, and black opaque stockings underneath. I immediately felt underdressed and a little annoyed that Cassandra hadn't made me aware of the more posh dress code. I saw her smile and reach her hand out to a tall guy wearing a dark blazer and a burgundy button-down. He had dark-brown, almost black, hair and chestnut- colored eyes. He looked a few years older than us and right away I knew this must be the new guy in her life.

"This is Brandon," she beamed. "Brandon, this is my oldest friend Amalia. Oh! And this is her friend from graduate school,

Olivia."

I wondered when I had been demoted from best friend to "oldest" friend. It must have been around the same time she went nearly two weeks without contacting me. I let out a soft sigh and longed for the days when we told each other everything.

"Hi," Olivia gave a small wave. Her eyes were downcast. She had told me earlier that she and Alex had barely spoken since their second fight in front of school. I had dragged her out to this party in an attempt to take her mind off things.

"Nice to meet you," I held out my hand. Cassandra gave Brandon a quick kiss on the cheek and then winked at me.

"It's nice to meet you both," he shook my hand firmly. "So, where do you two go to school?"

I was a little taken aback by the question. Surely Cassandra had mentioned where I went to school at least once.

"We go to NYU," I answered. I searched his face for a glimmer of recognition. There was none.

I turned back to Cassandra, who was already deep in conversation with a pretty brunette woman in her mid-forties. I assumed it was her boss. Olivia looked down at her feet and then back up at me. I smiled nervously and then turned back to Brandon. I opened my mouth to ask him about his job, but by the time I did he was already talking to someone else.

"Remind me again why we came to this thing?" Olivia asked, leading me to the bar.

"Because I was foolish enough to believe that Cassie wanted me here." I answered solemnly. "And because I thought it would be a good idea to mingle and get your mind off Alex. I'm sorry." I shrugged. "At least the drinks are free."

I looked around at the crowded venue. There were so many people laughing, shaking hands, and buying each other drinks. To the untrained eye, it appeared completely normal. Like any other Saturday night festivities. But to me it just looked utterly vacuous. Almost staged.

"Can you get me a rum and coke?" Olivia asked while digging through her purse. "I'm just going to go to the bathroom."

"You're going outside to smoke, aren't you?" I asked with a smirk.

"Shut up," she smiled and blew me a kiss. "I love ya."

I laughed and turned to the bartender, who was surprisingly not overwhelmed with patrons.

"What can I get you?" he asked, sounding slightly annoyed. I couldn't blame him, I wouldn't want to be serving these people all night either.

"Can I get a rum and coke and also a Jack and ginger?"

"Coming right up," he grabbed the rum and then walked to the other end of the bar to retrieve the whiskey.

"You're not drinking both of those yourself are you?" asked a voice from behind me. I rolled my eyes. I was not in the mood to get hit on.

"Nope," I answered without turning around. "One's for my friend." I really wasn't in the mood to get hit on.

"You sure, Amalia? I bet you could handle it."

I turned around just as someone bumped into Michael, forcing the two of us to collide. Even in small kitten heels I was as clumsy as ever.

"Are you alright?" Michael asked, holding onto my shoulders so I wouldn't fall.

"What are you doing here?" I asked, ignoring his question. I hated being in such close proximity with him. Mainly because as soon as our skin touched, I immediately felt flushed. I could feel my face burning and quickly lowered my head so my hair would cover my cheeks.

"I'm here with Angela," he answered coyly. "As her date."

I instantly straightened myself out and smoothed down my shirt. "Oh," was all I could muster.

"You look really nice," he smiled. I couldn't help but notice he looked really nice himself. Like most of the people there, he was more dressed up than usual. He had on a tailored black suit with a crisp baby-blue shirt, and a Burberry patterned tie.

"Here are your drinks, ma'am," spat out the bartender. I reached for them and shot him a look as I took a sip. Great, on top of everything else now I was being called *ma'am*.

"Where is she?" I stammered. I couldn't help but feel jealous. The entire time Michael and I were hooking up, he always belonged to someone else. He had never taken me as his date to anything. And I guess he never would.

"Who? Angela?" he asked, motioning for the bartender to come back around. "I think she's in the bathroom."

A moment later, Olivia and Angela walked out of the bathroom, laughing with each other like they had just heard the funniest thing in the world. Angela gave Olivia a light punch on the arm and Olivia wiped under her eyes where her eye make-up had ran from laughing so hard.

"Hey, look who I found!" Olivia said brightly. Her entire mood had livened up. I felt a pang of jealousy.

"Hi, Amalia," Angela smiled without looking at me. Maybe I was imagining it, but there was a certain hint of pride in her voice. Almost like she thought she was winning.

"Hey. I didn't know you'd be here," I said as politely as I could. I handed Olivia her drink and took another sip of mine.

"Yeah, I always go to these parties," she uttered nonchalantly. Like Cassandra, she too was dressed up. She wore a bright-red dress, patent-leather Tory Burch flats, and her hair was frizz-free and glistening with stage-worthy curls. Her dark skin looked flawless against the bright color, which only added to my insecurities about my own choice of outfit. "My friend Deacon is a model and he always tells me about these things."

"Oh," I mumbled. "That's lucky."

Olivia must have noticed my uncomfortable demeanor, because the next thing I knew she was dragging me outside with her.

"We'll be right back!" she ushered me to the front door, and I quickly placed my drink on a neighboring table. Olivia had already downed hers. Michael and Angela exchanged a confused look, but I ignored it. We fought our way past the crowd of twenty-somethings hanging outside until we reached the corner. The air was getting cooler. Even just a few days ago I would have been fine in a tank top. Now I felt like I needed a sweater.

"What are you doing?" I pulled away from her grasp.

"Where's your phone?" she asked, looking me dead in the eyes.

"It's in my purse," I raised a curious eyebrow. "Why?"

"Because you're drowning in there," she said sympathetically. "Now I want you to get out your phone and call Hayden."

"What?" I rolled my eyes. "No, Olivia. I'm not going to lead him on like that."

"It's either that or we leave," she ordered. "Because you are going to be miserable all night, and I'm already miserable about Alex, so we can't *both* be miserable. So get on your phone and ask that boy what he's doing tonight and give Michael a taste of his own medicine."

"This is so juvenile," I muttered as I dug through my handbag. "Are you drunk?"

As I plucked out my phone. It began to vibrate with a message from Hayden. Olivia looked over and laughed. "Its fate!" she nudged me. "And no, I'm not drunk. Yet."

I shook my head and began to type back.

"What did you say?" Olivia peered over my shoulder. She was nearly jumping up and down at this point, so clearly anxious to play match-maker.

"I just told him where I was and asked him if he wanted to hang out," I answered in a breezy tone. "I'm sure he already has plans, though."

A moment later my phone lit up with another message from Hayden. I smiled and began typing back.

"Let me guess," Olivia goaded. "He isn't busy and he'll be right here."

"Something like that," I nodded. I couldn't help but feel a little giddy. Hayden was a great guy. He was fun and easy to talk to. At the very least he'd make this party more enjoyable. Plus, there was always the added bonus of maybe making Michael jealous. "He's coming from a friend's apartment.

"So he left somewhere else to come hang out with you?" Olivia practically squealed. "It must be love."

"No," I laughed, dropping my phone back into my purse. "He must be bored. Now let's go back inside. I want to try to grab Cassie's attention again. I really want to try and re-connect with her if I can."

"Good luck with that," Olivia mumbled as she held the door open for me.

Within the ten minutes that Olivia and I were outside, the bar managed to house at least 30 more people. Fortunately, Cassandra was still hanging out in the back of the bar and I was able to spot her right away.

"I'm just going to make a phone call," Olivia said over the now louder music. "I'll be right back."

I nodded and told her where I'd be. I made my way through a mob of sparkly dresses and ill-fitting suits. From what I could hear of the conversations, it was a chorus of men poorly delivering one-liners to bored-looking women. As I continued to make my way to Cassandra, I kept getting knocked into on every side. No one even bothered to look up or say excuse me.

"Cassie!" I tapped her on the shoulder and she spun around.

"Hey, honey! Are you having fun?" she sounded, but her eyes told me a different story. They seemed distracted and vacant.

"Sure," I lied through a wide smile. "This is a pretty huge turnout. What is this party for anyway?" More people knocked into me as I tried to hold Cassandra's attention.

"It's for my boss's boss, who got a big promotion," she looked up and nodded, making sure she got the order right. "So now my boss, Leighton, has been promoted too, and the magazine is

93

actually looking for someone else to promote to her old position!"

"So does that mean you're up for the promotion?" I asked, genuinely excited for her.

"It's why I've been working all of those late nights. But then again, so has everyone else."

"That's fantastic!" I pulled her in for a hug. "Maybe we can get an early lunch tomorrow and you can tell me all about it before I move into my new apartment in the afternoon."

Cassandra's eyes glazed over and her attention started to shift toward someone behind me. She giggled and gave them a small wave. I turned around, but couldn't tell who she was communicating with.

"Sweetie, I'd love to," she answered quickly. "But I actually already have plans. Sometime next week?"

"Sure," I answered weakly. "Whenever you're free."

"Thanks, hun!" she spun on her heel and darted toward a tall red-head in the middle of the crowd. I heard her say something in Italian to the woman, and soon they were completely out of ear shot.

The room suddenly felt smaller as more and more people flooded in. Out of the corner of my eye, I saw Michael talking to Angela. She was leaning in toward him, playing with her long, dark hair. I felt my stomach drop as I watched him smile brightly at her. I was resolved to call it a night when I found Hayden sandwiched in between two hipsters. When he noticed me, he gently nudged past them and gave me a hug. I felt so relieved to see him.

"Wow," he looked around the room. "This is some shindig you were invited to."

"It's horrible," I widened my eyes. "Do you want to get out of here?"

He looked around one more time and then smiled.

"Absolutely."

Chapter 14

Olivia

I looked in through the window at everyone having the time of their lives at this party, but all I felt was alone. Worst off, I hated myself for it. When had I become so needy?

I hated fighting with Alex. I should be out enjoying this type of thing, but instead he had my mind all twisted up in terrible scenarios of what he might be doing, and who he might be doing it with. I tried his cell phone one more time. It rang three times and then the voicemail picked up. I refused to leave another voicemail. I didn't want to enter desperate territory. Even if it was how I felt.

The door to the bar swung open and out came Amalia and Hayden, their eyes darting around like they were sneaking out of classes early. Hayden pointed to the subway entrance across the street and Amalia nodded.

"Hey! Where are you two going?" I scampered over to them. "Are you just stepping outside for some air?"

Amalia's face turned white. Hayden blushed and looked at Amalia for help.

"Um, no. We're actually leaving," she shrugged her shoulders. I crossed my arms and she bashfully looked down at the ground.

"Wait a minute, you're leaving?" I said in a deflated voice. "It was your idea to come here."

"I know it was my idea to come here," she continued. "And I'm sorry but I can't stay here and be ignored by Cassandra *and* be upset by Michael any longer."

"Who's Michael?" Hayden crossed his arms defensively.

"No one," Amalia and I said in unison.

"Fine," I conceded. "I don't know what's going on with Cassandra either. She's not being a very good friend to you right now. I guess I'll just see you when you get back to my place tonight."

"Of course," she smiled. "It's the last night until I move into my new fabulous square box tomorrow."

"It's better than sleeping on a couch," Hayden chimed in. "No offence to your couch, Olivia. I'm sure it's lovely."

"Thanks," I said. "I guess."

I shot Amalia another look. She'd have to be blind and deaf not to know Hayden was into her. He left his friends to come straight here to see her, and how he was leaving the party without question. She was basically dragging him around like a loyal puppy, and from where I stood, he loved it.

"You know it occurs to me, Hayden, that we haven't been officially introduced," I said in a mocking tone. "Although you do look kind of familiar."

"Where are my manners?" Amalia spoke in an over-the-top, southern accent. She touched the tips of her fingers to her chest and proceeded to imitate our professor. "May I present to you my dear friend Olivia Davis. Olivia, this fine young man is Hayden. Maybe he looks familiar because y'all both went to the same university."

"Nice to finally meet you, Hayden!" We were all laughing at Amalia's impression of Dr. Greenfield. "Do you have a last name?"

"I sure do, little lady." Hayden tipped a pretend hat. By now the three of us were hysterically laughing. I had to admit I was on team Hayden for the win. Even from what little I knew of the guy, he was a hundred times easier to talk to than Michael. That had to count for something.

Just then, the door to the bar re-opened and out strolled Michael and Angela side by side. Amalia stopped laughing as he swiftly hailed a cab, and then held the door open for her. She subtly flipped her hair before carefully lowering herself into the vehicle. Michael walked across to the other side of the cab and caught eyes with Amalia. I watched as she tried to keep her composure, but if I looked closely enough I could see tears forming. He gave us a small wave before opening the car door and letting himself into the cab. The two of them drove off and for a moment Amalia just stood there, motionless.

Hayden gently reached for her shoulder and he spun around.

"Woah," he took a step back. "Are you okay? Who were those people?"

"They're just classmates," she uttered in a near-whisper.

"Is that all?" he asked, keeping his hand on her shoulder.

"I should let you two talk," I hiked my purse higher on my shoulder and pulled my metro card from my back pocket.

"Are you going home?" Amalia asked.

"I will be," I nodded. "But first, I'm going to hunt down Alex. I'm going to swing by his apartment and see if he's home. I'm getting tired of this radio-silence crap. Him and I are talking tonight, whether he likes it or not."

Chapter 15

Amalia

Hayden and I skipped the subway and aimlessly wandered around the city instead. I wasn't sure what neighborhood I was in. I knew I was downtown, but I had gotten mixed up somewhere around Alphabet City. Everything was still open so I wasn't nervous about not knowing where I was. Anytime we walked past a bar or a restaurant, a gust of air-conditioning would hit us, followed by a few chords of whatever song was playing inside.

"I'm sorry you left your friend's place to come out," I started. "I know I wasn't much fun tonight." I was growing more and more annoyed at Cassandra's aloofness. I had left the bar without saying goodbye to her, but chances were she hadn't even noticed. I had a strange, unsettling feeling in the pit of my stomach. But I couldn't deny, walking in the moonlight with Hayden definitely softened the blow of seeing Michael with Angela.

"I didn't mind it at all," he offered. "I see them fairly often. Besides, Jolene and Marc are a married couple, and she's pregnant. They were about to call it a night."

"You have friends that are already married?" I asked. "Are they a lot older than you?"

"No. Same age as me," he said as we stepped over a sewer grate. "Twenty-seven."

"I guess that's not so young, then," I realized. I thought back to Michael at the bar and wondered how old he would be when he got married. If ever. I shivered a bit as the wind kicked up.

"Time moves slower here," Hayden said. "Anyway, let's walk this way." He put his hand on the small of my back and led me toward First Avenue.

"What do you mean by that?" I asked, confused by his comment. "Have we accidentally slipped into some sort of vortex that I am unaware of?

"No, silly girl. I mean living in New York is like constantly living with the lights turned off on reality," he sighed.

"That's incredibly dramatic," I laughed. I didn't mean to come off rude, but I had no idea what he meant. "Honestly, Hayden, that sounds impossibly tragic."

"Let me explain," he offered as we made our way up First Avenue, passing St. Marks Place. "Think of New York City as this shiny object that you're distracted by."

"Uh huh," I said, trying to follow along. "And I am like a cat in this scenario?"

"Just bear with me," he laughed. "It can be incredibly enthralling to live here. Between all of the culture, the fashion, the new restaurants opening up, going to work or going to school, you are constantly in motion. You are constantly on the hunt for the next thing. You're always left in a state of *want*. I want that job, or I want that guy or girl." He paused for a moment, and then looked up at the sky. "Or I want to be the person I always imagined I would be once I moved here."

I looked over at Hayden. The smile had left his face and it was replaced with a serious look. His eyes were slightly narrowed and forehead was scrunched up. He rubbed his temples and continued.

"You don't realize the other things in life that you should be thinking about or noticing. Like how old you're getting, for example. You become so engrossed by the constant upkeep of it all. But no matter what you do, you'll never catch up. Because

101

secretly, you don't want to. You never let yourself feel, you know, relaxed. You never feel finished. And I don't know about you, but I don't know if I can honestly say I've grown a single day while living here. So yeah, it might seem weird to most people here that they're married and they are only twenty-seven, but I think it's wonderful. It's the first real thing any of my friends have done in a while. The first non-selfish thing."

Hayden's words hit me in a way I didn't expect. He had a point. I was going to be twenty-four this year and I really didn't feel like my life was any different than it was a year ago. To be fair, I was still in school and still living in the same city. How much could I really have expected it to change? And the real question, did I really want it to?

"I guess I know where you're coming from," I said in a comforting tone. "Manhattan's definitely a lot different now than it was when I was a kid. It used to be thought of as all Broadway and Bergdorf's. Now it's better known for cronuts and crack-houses."

Hayden let out a deep, throaty laugh. "And hipsters."

I smiled, happy to break him out of his temporary melancholy. "Do you know where I like to go when I feel that way?" I said. "You have to promise you won't make fun of me when I tell you. It's kind of touristy."

"You go to school by Washington Square Park," he said. "How much more touristy can it get?"

"I'm serious!" I laughed. "Although I have to admit, the view from the Kimmel student center is like something out of a movie. But I go somewhere even more touristy than that when I need a little inspiration."

"Do I strike you as the type of person who would make fun of you for something like that?" Hayden gave me a side smile as we continued our walk. "Here, turn up on 2nd Avenue."

I followed him up the street and a light gust of wind blew my hair back. I laughed as I picked strands of untamed blonde from my face.

"Okay, as long as you promise not to make fun of me I'll tell you. When I start to feel really somber, or lost, I wait until the sun goes down and I go sit in Zucotti Park."

"Isn't that in the Financial District?" he asked. I could tell he was getting cold too because he stood up a little straighter and dug his hands into his pants pockets.

"That's the one," I said, suddenly remembering being a child and walking around the city with my family. Flashbacks of Aaron always wanting to hold my hand because he felt so overwhelmed by it all. But not me, I always loved it here. My parents would take pictures of me in front of the bull statue, and we'd spend the afternoon walking around Battery Park or South Street Seaport. "My dad used to work on Wall Street before his company moved his department to their Midtown office. So when I was a little girl, he used to take me here for 'take your daughter to work day'. You know, that antiquated 'holiday' where girls didn't go to school for a day, but instead were taken to work by their fathers to help implement them to the working world? We would have to take the bus or the ferry to get here. The commute was absolutely horrible!"

Hayden laughed and started to slow down a bit. "First of all, they've changed it to 'take your *child* to work day' since then. It sounds more politically correct that way. Also, this story sounds terrible."

The neighborhood was becoming more residential and the streets were growing a little dimmer with each passing block. I hadn't seen a group of people walking on the same street with us for a few minutes now. Still, I felt comfortable with him by my side.

"It's not all bad," I said in a reassuring voice. "I always looked forward to it. For starters it got me out of school for the day, so I couldn't complain that much. Except for the fact that it was always in winter. I mean it was freezing getting into the city 6:30 am! Waiting for the bus in that weather was brutal. I had a new-found respect for my dad after I realized he had to do it every single day. But if we hadn't gotten into the city that early, then I

103

never would have seen them."

"Seen what?" Hayden asked, his stride had now turned into a leisurely stroll.

"The twinkling lights in the park. The ones that illuminate the steps. They were always still on from the night before, but the whole area was completely empty at that time of day. It was so beautiful. I remember being eight years old, turning to my dad and saying that one day I wanted to live here. I want to live somewhere that made me feel that exhilaration."

"That's a beautiful story," he said, without a hint of sarcasm. "I wish I still felt that way about this city."

"You don't?" I asked, surprised by his openness.

"It changes," he offered. "Some days I wake up, look out my window and think, my God have you ever seen anything so amazing? Other days I just wish I could get in my car and drive until I hit a beach and never come back."

I wanted to say something positive, but couldn't think of anything. I glanced around and noticed we had stopped walking.

"Wait, why did we stop walking? Where are we?" I looked around. But as soon as I saw the street sign, I knew. "When did we turn onto 3rd Avenue?"

"Somewhere between the twinkling lights and 33rd Street," Hayden joked.

"Wow. We must have been walking for–"

"About 40 minutes," he cut me off, as he checked his watch. "What can I say? I wanted to be the first person to see your new apartment. Besides Olivia, of course."

"Well here it is!" I pointed to the bleak brown building in the middle of 33rd and 34th Street. "412, 3rd Avenue."

"What floor are you on?" he asked, studying the building.

"The third," I shrugged. "It's not exactly the Ritz, but it's all I can afford. And if Professor Greenfield doesn't let me into his research study soon, I'll be roommates with that homeless person we passed back on 22nd Street." I looked back up at the building and for a brief moment, felt a pang of sadness for my old apartment. "I can't believe I am moving in tomorrow. I should really get back to Brooklyn and get some sleep."

I looked around for a subway entrance, but there was none in sight. Just then, Hayden took me by the shoulders and looked me right in the eyes. He brushed a long strand of hair from my face that had been tousled in the wind.

"Amalia, I have to be honest here," he began. "I like you. I like you as more than a friend, and I have liked you from the first day I met you. I guess what I'm trying to ask you here, is would you go out with me? On a real date?"

Even in the chilly night air, I could feel my face and neck growing warmer. I was shocked. The last person I heard speak so declaratively about their own feelings was Nicholas. But this felt completely different. Hayden was nothing like Nicholas. He was an adult. It was something I could feel the moment I met him. In a city where everyone was so hard to read, Hayden was completely comfortable letting me know what he was thinking. I looked back into his eyes, so full of hope. Hope that I would say yes to him. And I had to admit it felt good being the one on the receiving end of the chase. I racked my brain, trying to come up with a good reason not to say yes to him. I could tell him I wasn't looking for a boyfriend right now, or I could unleash all of my pent-up emotions about Michael and how he made me feel last year. The fact of the matter was, I couldn't deny I had feelings for Hayden. Feelings that had grown stronger with each step we took on this walk. A part of me didn't want any more pain. I didn't want to receive any and I didn't want to cause any. So I opened my mouth to let him down gently. But I didn't do that. Instead, I smiled and said yes. Hayden bent down slightly and softly moved both of his hands to my face. And right there, in front of my new home-to-be, he kissed me under the twinkling lights in the sky.

Chapter 16

Olivia

Taking a cab from downtown Manhattan to Roosevelt Island wasn't exactly an option for me, considering I thought I'd be spending the night at a party where all of the drinks were free, and I had exactly four dollars in my wallet. I knew I had enough money on my metro card, and the sky tram had already stopped running for the night, so I hiked to the nearest subway entrance nearly four blocks away and prayed there was an F train running. As I descended the stairs that were for some reason wet, even though it hadn't rained in days, I noticed a familiar face waiting on the platform. It was my old college boyfriend, Nate. I knew it was him immediately. He was the only grown man in New York City wearing flip-flops, khaki shorts, a short sleeve T-shirt and a brightly colored button-down on top of it. Or, as I liked to call it, the Florida Uniform. He was standing by himself, nodding along to whatever he was playing off his iPhone. He was seemingly unaware of his surroundings.

I thought about ignoring him for a moment, but I was too curious as to what he was doing in Manhattan. I couldn't help it. I walked right up to him and tapped him on the shoulder.

"Olivia?" he asked, plucking the ear buds out of his ears. "Holy crap, it is you!" He pulled me in for a big hug and lifted me off the ground.

"What are you doing here? Are you on vacation" I asked. I couldn't help but smile. Nate and I had ended things on good enough terms and it was nice to see him.

"I'm in town for about a week," he nodded. "Believe it or not, I've never been to New York before." He wrapped his headphones tightly around his phone and slipped everything into his over-sized back pocket.

His hair was blonder than I remembered, but he still looked like the same Nate I knew back in college. He was still very thin, perpetually tan, same tattoo on his forearm (although the constant time in the sun had faded the coloring), and still about five foot eight with crystal-clear blue eyes.

"That's right. You used to say that all of the time," I laughed. I could remember Nate and I sitting in my dorm room at the University of Florida. I had one of those spinning globes on my desk and on Friday nights we would always drink SoCo and joke that wherever our finger landed we would have our next adventure. Of course, Nate was all talk and no action when it came to adventure. He was a townie for life. He had never left his hometown of Gainesville for more than a few days, and certainly had never been outside of America. In fact, this week-long trip to New York was probably the longest vacation he'd ever been on.

"And you always rubbed it in my face how you were going to live here one day," he countered. "I guess you made that happen for yourself."

It had been one of the reason's Nate and I broke up. He was completely comfortable staying put, but after college I knew I wanted to move up to New York. I wanted out of my town. Not that there was necessarily anything wrong with living there. I just felt like I could grow so much more in a big city. Maybe wanting to live here had partially been influenced by movies and books, but once I was accepted to NYU for graduate school, I knew there was no turning back.

There was an awkward silence that fell on us as we both simultaneously remembered the reason why we had fought for nearly a week straight, and then finally agreed that the best thing for both of us would be to move on. We agreed to stay friends, but lost touch almost immediately after graduation. We weren't even friends on Facebook.

I heard a loud sound echoing in the background and could see the train's headlights making their way around the corner. I breathed a sigh of relief when the letter F appeared illuminated on the front of the train.

"Yeah, I moved here when I started graduate school," I said, unsure if I should let him in on how happy I was to live here. I had no idea what he had been doing with his life since college, and I didn't want to rub it in that my dream had come true if he was working at a Cracker Barrel. "I live in Brooklyn, in a neighborhood called Park Slope. But actually I am going to hop on this train and pay a visit to my boyfriend."

"You have a boyfriend?" he asked, his voice going up at the end. "A New Yorker?"

The train came to a screeching halt and the doors swung open. A barely audible announcement was made over the speakers and I stepped aside to let the flood of passengers get off first before hopping on.

"His name is Alex," I smiled. "He lives in another part of the city, but he's not from New York." At least I thought I still had a boyfriend. After a few days without a decent conversation, I was beginning to wonder if our relationship status had changed. I inched closer to the door as the last passenger hurried off the train. Finally, the last person exited and I hopped onto the train.

"My number's still the same," Nate called to me as I hung onto the railing. "Call me if you want to get together this week. Maybe you can show me around?"

Before I could answer, there was a loud ding and the doors closed. I waved at Nate as he patiently waited on whatever subway line he was there for.

By the time I got to Roosevelt Island, it was around 10:30. Alex's phone went straight to voicemail for the third time as I made my way down Main Street and arrived in front of his apartment building. I had been there enough times to be able to bypass the doorman without suspicion, and in the beginning of the summer Alex had given me my own set of keys.

When I got to the door of his apartment, I reached into my purse for the keys but was surprised to find that I didn't need them. The door was slightly open and from what I could see all of the lights were on. The first thing I felt was panic. Did someone break into Alex's apartment?

Then I heard his voice. I breathed a sigh of relief but stopped myself from walking inside when I heard another voice. One I didn't recognize.

"What were you doing that was so important that you had to make me look like a fool when you never showed up for lunch?" the voice boomed. "You know I am only here for a few days, my time is very limited."

"Well I'm so sorry to be such an inconvenience," Alex retorted. "If you're really so hard- pressed for time, perhaps you should just stay home next time."

Standing by the door, I listened to Alex and quickly realized he was arguing with his father. I felt helpless, completely unable to help him. I also felt a little nervous and wondered if I should just walk away now and pretend like I had never been here. I reached into my purse and flipped my phone on silent. I had seen people get caught spying way too many times when their phone began to ring. There was no way that was going to happen to me.

"I came here for work and I thought it would be nice if we could spend some time together," his father was practically yelling.

"Let's be serious here," Alex voice was also reaching a near-bellow. "You *came* here for work, and you felt obligated to see your

110

son, who you have barely contacted in the past year and a half."

I was proud of Alex for finally standing up to his father. The man had way too much control over his son's emotions. I always wondered what his dad had on him that made Alex keep going back for more.

As I leaned closer to the door, I accidentally put too much weight on it and the door ended up swinging open. I fell forward and regained my footing but not before my purse slammed onto the floor. My lipstick rolled halfway across the room until finally it landed right beside Alex's foot. I had landed in a crouched-down position and was now looking up toward both of them. His father and he finally stopped yelling long enough to cock their heads at me.

"Um, hi," I gave a small wave and a weak smile.

Alex just rubbed his temples and shook his head. I walked over to him to retrieve my lipstick, but he bent down and picked it up for me.

"What are you doing here?" he asked me in a low voice.

Slowly, I looked over at his father. He stood tall at about six foot one, was wearing a perfectly tailored midnight-blue suit and the crispest white shirt I had ever seen. His tie was flawlessly knotted and held back with a shiny silver tie clip.

"I was worried about you," I apprehensively stood up. "You weren't answering your phone." I glanced over to his father, whose face was red with anger. "But I see that you're in the middle of something, so I should go."

"Yes, young lady. You should go," Alex's dad said to me with folded arms. I felt a wave of anger. This man hardly knew me at all. He had no right to talk to me like this. Just because Alex was too afraid to stand up to his dad, definitely didn't mean I was. But before I could open my mouth to tell him how I really felt about him, Alex completely surprised us and beat me to it.

"Don't you dare talk to her like that," he said in an eerily calm voice. He lifted his index finger and pointed it in his father's face.

He looked him straight in the eyes and then pointed to his door. "In fact, I think you're the one who should go."

"You be careful, young man," his father snapped. "You want to keep living in this apartment? Then you had better show me some respect."

I knew Alex's family paid for him to live in his apartment, but I never knew there were strings attached. Suddenly it all made sense. The reason why Alex got so rattled every time he had to see his father. It was clear that his dad was trying to control him. For a moment Alex looked like he didn't know what to say. His father's mouth twisted into a self-satisfying smile. Alex repeated his request for his dad to leave and without another word, he finally did.

"I'm sorry I just barged in like this," I said, as soon as the door closed. "But I didn't know what else to do. You weren't answering my calls. It's been days since we've had a real conversation. I was worried about you. About us."

Alex walked over to me and hugged me. First soft and lightly, then more tightly. I felt like crying, but held it in.

"I'm sorry," he whispered into my hair. I pulled out of his embrace to look in his eyes, but he kept his arms around me the entire time. "I should have listened to you about my dad. If him being here has taught me anything it's what an asshole he can truly be."

"I'm sorry if I pushed you too hard," I said, unable to look away from him. "But you can never scare me like that again."

He leaned in and softly kissed me. Running his fingers over my face and then through my hair. He broke away and whispered "I never will."

"I love you," I pulled him in for another kiss. He lifted me up and carried me over to the bedroom.

"I love you too, sweetheart," he said and he lightly tugged on my top.

He touched my bottom lip and I couldn't help but yank his shirt right off. A few moments later, we were under the covers, making love. I was completely happy again.

Chapter 17

Amalia

"Table for two, please," I said to the hostess at Spring Street Natural down in SoHo. She grabbed two leather-bound menus from under a podium and motioned for me to follow her to a table. I had finally gotten Cassandra to agree to meet me for lunch. Our relationships had become extremely strained. For the first time ever, I was nervous to hang out with my best friend.

Even though she worked in Chelsea, Cassie told me she had a meeting in SoHo at around 2 o'clock, and that she was carving out her whole lunch hour beforehand to meet with me. The restaurant was well known for their delicious tomato bread and all-organic menu. I didn't get the chance to mention to Cassandra that I had a meeting myself, to pick up my work-study forms at 2:30 and would have to leave at the same time anyway. I didn't know whether to feel happy that she was going out of her way to see me, or annoyed at her for making me feel like her time was more significant than mine. Either way, I decided to keep positive and just see what kind of mood she was in.

The hostess showed me to a booth by the window and told me my server would be right with me. As I sat and waited for Cassie, my phone vibrated with a text from Hayden asking how my day was going. I couldn't help but smile.

Hayden and I had gone out on one official date since he first kissed me in front of my new apartment building, and it was fantastic. Both the date and the kiss. He took me to this great Italian restaurant in Hell's Kitchen that I had never even heard of before. It was nice to get out of the downtown bubble and explore more aspects of the city. Hayden picked me up at my apartment in a cab that drove us up to the restaurant. I had only been living there a couple of weeks. It was slowly coming together. When we got to the restaurant, the food was delicious, and he had even ordered a bottle of Merlot for us to split. I was too embarrassed to tell him that it was the first time I had ever really been on an official date, and my knowledge of wine began and ended with two-buck-chuck from Trader Joe's. Michael and I had definitely never gone on a real date. Everything we did was always so convoluted. Always in secret. When Nick and I were together, we would usually just hang out at his apartment and order Thai take out. But everything I did with Hayden was different. It just felt more adult.

When we finished dessert and the check came, he refused to let me pay (which was a relief because I was completely broke), and he told the cab to drop me back off at my apartment. He kissed me goodnight and asked me if I was free the following weekend. Two perfect kisses in total. The whole experience was new to me. For starters, we went out on dates in public. Right there was an instant upgrade. Secondly, I already knew he had feelings for me. There was no late-night anxiety or urgent crying phone calls to my friends. No debriefings with Olivia to try and uncover the hidden subtext of his latest Facebook status. For example, were those song lyrics about me? Or did he just have that Radiohead song stuck in his head? And third, he was completely adorable.

I texted back that I was waiting for Cassandra to meet me for lunch. As soon as I hit send, I was greeted with the familiar sound of heels clanking on the floor. I looked up and saw Cassie walking toward me. She had her cell phone in her left hand, firmly pressed to her ear, and a red Tory Burch clutch in her right hand.

I mouthed the word "hey" as she approached the table, but she just smiled and put up one finger, instructing me that she'd be off the phone in just a moment.

I took the opportunity to write to Hayden and ask him what he had in mind for the upcoming weekend. He wrote back one word, *bowling*. I felt my face scrunch up and told myself that he must be joking.

"What's with the face?" Cassandra said as she pulled out her chair. "Oh, let me guess, Michael drama?"

Her blonde hair was tied back into a tight ponytail. She had on a purple button-down blouse with black, skinny jeans and her signature four-inch heels. A crystal statement piece hung around her neck and her nails were perfectly manicured a light ballet pink. She was dressed like she meant business. As she sat down she carefully placed her cell phone right next to her water glass. God forbid she leave it in her pocket or purse, which is exactly where I placed mine after she made that comment.

"No, I haven't even seen him since that night at the bar," I said coolly. "When he left with Angela." I still wasn't quite sure what was going on between the two of them. Or why I let it bother me.

"Which night?" Cassandra asked as she scanned the menu.

"The night we all went out to that bar for your boss's party about two weeks ago," I picked up the menu and rolled my eyes behind it, then subtly lowered it back down. I wanted to gauge her reaction, see if she was upset with me for leaving that night without saying goodbye to her. I hadn't spoken to her since that night, and Cassandra had paid such little attention to me I had no idea whether or not she even realized I had left early.

"Oh okay," was all she said.

The waitress walked up to us and asked what we'd like to drink. She was dressed in all black, with a short pixie-cut hairstyle.

"I'll have a Cabernet," Cassandra said without looking up from her menu.

"Pinot Grigio. Thank you."

After the waitress walked away, I put down my menu and tried to get Cassandra's attention.

"So," I started. "Brandon seemed nice, not to mention really cute. Are you two still seeing each other?"

"We are," she finally put the menu down and smiled. "I'm actually seeing him tonight."

"Nice!" I said, putting a little enthusiasm into my voice. "What are you two doing to do?"

"Not sure," she answered noncommittally. "We'll probably go to dinner somewhere in the Meat Packing District and then back to his place for some dessert."

"Real dessert?" I asked with a laugh. "Or *dessert* dessert?"

"What do you think?" she gave me a wink and then picked her menu back up.

"Are you two officially dating?"

"No, we're just having fun," she spoke in a cavalier fashion.

Well that conversation lasted two seconds, I thought. I took a sip of water and looked around at the crowd. A few people power-lunching, a few hipsters hanging out in between band practice, and a couple of uncomfortable day-dates. Cassandra seemed utterly distracted, and in between glances at the menu she kept checking her phone. I decided to tell her about Hayden to get her attention.

"Hayden made an appearance at that party too," I said, hoping to raise her curiosity. "We actually snuck out early and walked around downtown a little bit. We ended up walking all the way to my new apartment, which you totally need to come over and see, by the way. Anyway, I was so surprised at the end of the night when he kissed me."

"Good," she said in a matter-of-fact tone. "Hayden always seemed like a nice guy, even though Bryce was a total ass. Plus, last thing you need to do is start things back up with Michael. You and Hayden are a good fit."

"Who said anything about me starting things back up with Michael?" I asked, feeling slightly offended. "I've barely even spoken to him since the semester began."

"I didn't say you were going to," she back-pedaled. "I was just stating the obvious. That's all."

I pursed my lips together but she didn't notice. I hated that she would automatically assume I would jump back into bed with Michael. I wanted to tell her more about Hayden to prove to her that I wasn't thinking about Michael, but the waitress materialized as soon as I was about to ask her if she thought bowling was a good idea for a second date.

"What can I get for you ladies?" she handed us our drinks and pulled out a notepad from her back pocket.

"I'll have the Asian chicken salad with the dressing on the side," Cassandra said as she handed over her menu.

"I'll have the veggie burger and a side salad," I said, already knowing what I was going to order before I came. I always looked up the restaurant's menu online first. I hated wasting time going over it in the restaurant.

Cassandra reached for her wine while simultaneously checking her phone. She made a face and quickly began to type.

"What's wrong?" I asked. "Is it Brandon?"

"No. It's work," she explained. She grimaced and continued feverishly typing an email. "I am going to have to cut this lunch short."

"Wow, Cassie," I said with a sigh. "Don't you ever get sick of your job completely running your life?"

That got her attention. I couldn't help it. I knew what I said was rude, but this had been going on long enough. I'd been back for a month and could count on one hand how many times Cassandra and I had interacted since my return. I was beginning to wonder if she was alienating all of her friends, and if maybe this was a larger issue than her solely being consumed with her career. She carefully placed her phone on the table and widened her eyes. She ever so slightly bit her bottom lip, looking like she was carefully considering how she was going to answer me.

"What are you talking about, Amalia?" she said slowly. Measured. As if she was deliberately trying to stay calm.

"I'm talking about how unbelievably busy you've been this past month," I unleashed. "Cassandra, I have barely seen you since I got back and every time we hang out or speak, you have to cut out early because of something work-related. I understand that your job is important to you but you're constantly either ditching me, or you're glued to your phone the entire time. I know nothing about what's going on in your life right now, except for the morsels you throw me after I feel like I've interrogated them out of you. I don't even know who this guy you're dating is. You haven't even told me his last name." I shook my head in disbelief that I was even having this conversation with her. Cassandra used to run every move by me, just as I did with her. She was the person I told everything to. We had an unbreakable bond that our other friends were always jealous of, and now I felt like we were strangers. How could things have shifted so dramatically so quickly? I felt warm tears burning behind my eyes, but resolved to not let her see my cry over this. I took a deep breath and spoke more softly. "I just don't know how you can enjoy the type of job that expects you to be on call 24/7, and completely detach yourself from any other aspect of your life."

"I'm up for a promotion, I have to be pro-active," she calmly defended herself. The unflappable tone in her voice made me feel more uneasy than if she had thrown her glass of wine in my face. "Besides, you're still in school. You don't know what it's like to be this busy."

I recoiled from her arrogant comment. "Cassie, of course I know what it's like to be insanely busy," I shook my head in disbelief. "I am *constantly* swamped. I can't even do work for one class without worrying about what's due in another one. If I'm writing a paper in Social Psych, I spend the entire time thinking I should be studying for my Human Development class. Plus I am most likely going to be starting a new work-study program, *and* I just

120

moved into a new apartment, which by the way you haven't even seen yet. Cassandra, I am just as busy as you are. The difference is, I don't ignore you when we're together. And I definitely don't make you feel like I'm doing you a favor each time I grace you with my presence. I mean, come on! What happened to us being *best* friends?"

She just looked at me with narrowed eyes. Silence fell between us as her phone continued to vibrate, proving a point on both of our ends. The waitress walked over to us but Cassandra shot her a look and she changed directions and walked to a neighboring table.

"I'm sorry but I can't talk about this right now," she took a final sip of her wine and grabbed her clutch off the table. "I have to get to my meeting." She calmly placed some money on the table and then smoothed out her hair. "We can talk about this another time, Amalia." The formality in her voice made my blood boil.

"I'm sure we will," I said with added sarcasm. I knew I was being petty, but I couldn't help it. Now she was deciding when and where we had conversations too?

Cassandra just muttered something under her breath in Italian, turned on her heel and strutted out of the restaurant. I couldn't believe what had become of my friend. Once loud and vivacious, now stone-cold and repressed. I thought back to last Christmas, how close-knit she and I had been. Or just a few months ago, when we shared a box of Magnolia Bakery cupcakes as we commiserated over our guy troubles. Now she felt almost like a stranger to me. I sat in silence for a moment longer and then motioned to the waitress.

"Hi, it's just going to be me, actually. My friend had to leave. I'm sorry," I gave a weary smile.

"That's okay," she said, completely apathetic to the situation. "Your food will be right up."

Within seconds, a food runner came over with my veggie burger and I suddenly realized I was going to endure the awkward task of eating at a restaurant alone. I reached into my purse, hoping I

121

had left my Kindle in there. I hadn't. I cursed under my breath and then I realized there was one person who had seen Cassandra over the summer when I wasn't here. Someone who could possibly give me some insight as to why she was acting so detached. I grabbed my phone out of my purse and scrolled through my contacts. The phone rang twice before he finally picked up.

"Hello? Hey Aaron, it's me! How are you?"

Chapter 18

Olivia

"First test of the semester, babe. You ready for this?" Alex had his arm around me as we walked into the building. I felt like one of those old fifties couples that everyone wanted to be like. We had finally made up after his father left that night, and for the past few weeks we had been closer than ever. He was even joking about us moving in together last night before bed.

"I think I studied just about enough to get a solid B+," I answered with a nod.

"That's my girl," he laughed. He pulled me in closer and whispered in my ear, "I bet you'll get an A. You're destined for greatness. Plus you look really hot in that skirt."

I impulsively grabbed his collar and pulled him in for a kiss. He kissed me harder, and we took a few steps backwards until we knocked into a wall. His hand softly slid up the bottom of my shirt and I felt a rush of excitement. A few undergrads made cheering sounds and I pulled away as soon as I noticed one of my professors out of the corner of my eye. I cleared my throat and reached for Alex's hand.

"Let's get to class," I smiled. "Before we end up skipping it entirely." I was completely fine with everyone knowing Alex and I were in a relationship, but I didn't want the entire school gawking at us.

"Would that really be such a bad thing?" he winked and pulled me in closer.

"I think if we want to graduate on time, it would be a very bad thing."

Alex kept giving me the eyes as we made our way to the elevator. I playfully shoved him and giggled and, without looking, I collided with Angela.

"Sorry!" I felt my face turn red with embarrassment. "Are you okay?"

"I'll live," she laughed, regaining her composure. "How are you guys? I haven't seen you since the bar that night."

"We're good," Alex answered for me. His arm was still wrapped around my waist.

"What about you?" I asked, suddenly remembering she left the party with Michael that evening. "Is there something going on between you and Michael? I know you said he was your date to the party."

"Well, I-" she started, but then noticed Alex looking right at her, obviously just as interested in her answer as I was. It was hard to notice with her dark complexion, but I could see just the faintest hint of embarrassment on her face. She straightened herself out and gave us a full smile. "I should go upstairs and go over my notes one more time before this exam. But Olivia, do you want to get lunch this weekend?"

"Sure," I answered. "Give me a call tomorrow and we'll figure it out." I was glad she asked me to hang out. It was about time we got some answers about what she and Michael were up to.

Angela looked past us and then quickly said bye. I turned around and saw Amalia heading in our direction. By the time I looked back to say goodbye to Angela, she was already on the elevator, frantically hitting the door-close button.

"That friend of yours is a little weird," Alex muttered as Amalia came closer to us.

"I'm starting to notice that too."

"Pretty soon we'll be brunching on Sundays with her and Michael," Alex whispered.

"Shh. Don't say that."

"Hey guys," Amalia greeted us with a big smile. "Where did Angela go?"

"Not sure," I answered. "She had to run off. Why are you in such a good mood?"

Alex hit the up button on the elevator and Amalia began to tell us about her date with Hayden and how he asked her to go bowling with him this weekend.

"At Bowlmor?" Alex asked as we piled into the elevator.

"I think so," Amalia shrugged.

"Then you should absolutely go," he pressed the button for the third floor. "That place is awesome."

"It's pretty cool," I agreed. "It's usually adult-only at night, and they serve interesting cocktails right to your lane. Unless you're looking for reasons not to go out with him again?"

"Go out with who again?" Michael materialized just as we were about to board the elevator.

Amalia and I exchanged a quick glance and Alex went completely silent. Michael shifted his weight as he waited for someone to answer him.

"Go out with this guy Hayden that I know," Amalia finally answered. "We've only been on one date but he's asked me to go to Bowlmor with him this weekend."

I squeezed Alex's hand, a small way of telling him that I loved him and I was so glad we didn't ever have to have awkward conversations like these.

The elevator stopped at the third floor and we all exited together, Alex putting his hand in front of the door to make sure it didn't close on any of us.

"Sounds like fun," was all he said. He walked straight toward the classroom and scanned it for an empty row.

126

Amalia looked deflated. One wrong word from Michael and her whole demeanor had changed. I wondered when she was finally going to let him go.

"Yeah," she said with her head down. "It sure does."

"Almost as much fun as this exam's going to be, Hastings!" Alex chimed in with an over-the-top smile. "I definitely think you're going to turn it around this semester and surprise us all."

"You are so lucky you're my friend's boyfriend, Alex," Amalia said through tight lips. "Or I'd be forced to hate you."

"Likewise," he smiled.

I lightly hit Alex's shoulder and he defended himself by saying he was just joking.

"Don't you have your meeting with Dr. Greenfield when this test is over?" I turned to Amalia.

"Don't remind me," she rubbed her temples. "I have my work-study papers all in order to give in to him. But I'm pretty sure I could have three letters of recommendation, a copy of my transcript from Rutgers, and a signed note from my mommy saying what I good student I am, and that man is still going to eat me alive later."

"Just don't do your southern accent in front of him and you'll be fine," I chided.

When we entered the classroom, I saw Angela sitting at a desk, going through her notes like she said she would be. Michael led the way and sat down next to her. Amalia seemed to tense up as he lowered himself into the chair. The rest of us followed and filled out the remaining seats in the fourth row.

Before any of us could say another word, Dr. Greenfield walked down the row with a huge stack of papers in one hand and his old beat-up briefcase in the other. His T.A. followed him in complete silence, holding another large stack of papers. I could only assume those were our exam booklets. I felt a bead of sweat roll down my back.

"Please clear your desks of all study materials," Dr. Greenfield said loudly as he approached the lectern. "You have exactly one and a half hours to complete this exam. If you do not finish in the time allotted, then the questions you don't answer will be marked incorrect. You may begin as soon as you receive your test booklet."

"First exam of the semester. Here we go," I said, reaching in my bag for an extra pen. "Good luck everyone."

"Thanks, Olivia," Angela nodded. "We should probably do a group-study session before the next exam."

"Yeah. Thanks, Olivia," Amalia mumbled, ignoring Angela's comment. "I'm more nervous about my meeting with him after class."

"I heard he's notorious for not giving out anything higher than an A-," Alex said to all of us.

"You're all going to do fine," Michael said, unexpectedly. "Just relax."

Amalia and I smiled at each other.

"Thanks. Love you too, man," Alex patted him on the back.

We all started snickering and a few students turned around to look at us. I just shook my head and for a moment felt truly grateful to have these crazy people as my friends. I looked over at Alex and felt a warm fuzzy feeling that I could only identify as love. Finally, things were back on track.

"Okay," I said, receiving the test booklet from the T.A. "I'm ready."

Chapter 19

Amalia

"Believe it or not, I think I may have aced this one," Olivia declared as she handed her finished test booklet back to the T.A. "Want to go grab a drink and celebrate, babe?"

"Absolutely," Alex said with a wink. He and Michael were both in good spirits. I could tell they were thinking the same thing as Olivia. That the test was a piece of cake. Which only left myself and Angela, who was currently just staring at the floor at this point, in the minority. I almost felt sorry for her. She might have even done worse than I had.

Just as the last student handed in their finished exams, I stood up and gathered my belongings.

"Hey," Michael lightly touched my arm. "I don't have any other classes left today, do you want to get a cup of coffee when you get done talking to the professor?"

I paused for a moment, unsure of what to say. I glanced over at Angela to gauge her reaction, but she was still immobile. Before my brain could say no, my mouth told him I'd meet him at Grounded in an hour.

"That's on Jane Street, right?" he asked.

I looked back at him. His dark eyes flickered in the dimly lit classroom. He gave me the smallest hint of a smile as he waited for me answer. Why did he always have to look so sexy?

"Yes," I stammered. "See you in a bit."

I silently kicked myself for saying yes, but as soon as I approached the front of the room, a new fear set in. Dr. Greenfield was already packed up and waiting for me. It seemed my two-second conversation with Michael had been holding him up. His lips were pressed into a straight line, and as I stopped directly in front of him, he dramatically checked his watch.

"Ms. Amalia Hastings," he dragged out my full name in a long drawl.

"Yes, professor," I nodded. I fiddled with the clasp on my bag for a second, and his eyes immediately darted over to my hand. This man didn't miss anything.

He narrowed his eyes and stood up a little straighter. He was wearing black slacks and a grayish-green tweed jacket with brown patches over the elbows. His gait was strong and he held his head high. "Alright. Follow me," he motioned for me to start walking. We walked out of the classroom and about ten feet down the hallway until we reached a tucked-away strip of offices. The corridor was narrow, and from what I could see, had about six or seven offices inside. We were immediately greeted by a perky receptionist at the entrance, but Dr. Greenfield passed by her without so much as a grunt. I glanced around the doors of the offices and noticed the names of two of my professors from last year. This must be where they all went when they were hiding from us. He led me to his door, which was the last one in the corridor. It was set back, away from the receptionist and away from any windows. For a moment I felt sorry for him and wondered if he got lonely back here. As he fiddled with his key to unlock the door, I felt my phone buzz in my bag. Dr. Greenfield shot me a look and I let out a sharp, breathy laugh. "I'm sorry! I'm turning it off," I said, holding down the power button.

Entering his office, I took a quick look around. It was musty, obviously due to the lack of fresh air, but apart from that it was

131

in pristine condition. There was a red Persian rug on the floor to make the room cozier. Perfectly hung abstract art decorated the plain-white walls. On a small desk was a coffee-maker that was completely cleaned out. I wondered if he ever even used it or if he was so fastidious that he cleaned it after every pot he made. A single mug sat next to the coffee machine with the words Yale Alumni printed on it. I looked around his office some more and noticed his diplomas. He not only went to Yale for undergrad, but he had obtained his doctorate there also. I felt myself nod and realized that I should probably stop being afraid of this man and start listening to whatever it was he had to say. Dr. Greenfield ran his hand over his desk, unaware of my snooping.

"Do you have you work-study forms?" he asked, breaking me out of my daze. He took a seat behind his large, wooden desk and I scrambled to sit down in the black-leather chair that was positioned across from him.

"Yes," I said, trying to sound professional. "I have them right here." I reached into my computer bag and pulled out a plain manila folder, which housed most of my loose papers. As I handed them to Dr. Greenfield, he made an unidentifiable sound.

"Is everything alright with them?" I suddenly wondered if I forgot to fill out the back page.

"Yes," he neatly placed them on top of a file on his desk, in between a clock and one of those sand-filled hourglasses. "Everything appears to be in order. Now we can start the interview."

I placed my bag on the floor, crossed my legs, and sat up as straight as possible. "I'm ready."

"Well, Amalia, there is no doubt you qualify for eligibility on my program," he began. I knew that wasn't a compliment, but I still took the opportunity to smile. "Having said that, what I am really interested in is why you want to be a part of my research team. I am hoping it isn't merely to make a few extra bucks."

I tried not to laugh at the way he said the word bucks. I couldn't tell if he was being ironic or not.

"Well, sir, I have been reading up on the research you're doing with Observational Learning, and I find myself drawn to it," I announced. That was a lie. Sure I found it interesting enough, but I wouldn't say it was calling out to me in my sleep. "I also haven't gotten any research experience yet while I've been here at NYU, and I thought this research study would be a great opportunity for me."

Dr. Greenfield put his hands in the steeple position and rested his chin on top. He looked me up and down as he contemplated my response.

"Tell me, Ms. Hastings, what is it that you want to do with your life?" he leaned forward in his chair.

"What do you mean?" I asked. "Are you asking what I want to be when I grow up?"

"I mean once you graduate with your Master's degree, what do you want to do? Career-wise?" he continued, ignoring my joke.

"To be honest with you, I haven't settled on any one thing just yet," I said. It was the truth. There were many aspects of my field that I found interesting, but nothing had really reached out and grabbed me. I knew I didn't want to take any of the hard science classes, and the idea of being a therapist never really crossed my mind. I offered Dr. Greenfield a small smile. "But your class has definitely opened my eyes to the world of Social Psychology. Maybe one day I could become a professor like you."

He seemed utterly unimpressed with my answers. He merely kept glaring at me. Not that I expected a man with a degree from Yale to be impressed by the likes of me.

"Well, I'm glad you're at least starting to think about your future. Although most students here probably know what they wanted to do from the moment they first enrolled."

I took a deep breath and let it out slowly, trying to keep my anxiety at bay.

"If you are accepted in my research study, it will take up a good deal of your time."

"I know that," I said with a nod. "I mean, I'm prepared for that."

Dr. Greenfield gave me a nod, followed by a long, hard look. I tried my best to smile, even though I was terrified of this man. Being in school as an adult is so much more complicated than when you're younger. Even just a few years ago, when I was at Rutgers, I felt completely comfortable with the pecking order. When you're a child or a teenager, you just assume that your teachers know more than you. That they're, in some way, better than you. You have to listen to and respect them because at the time you're just a child and that's what you're taught. But when you're obviously smart enough to be in graduate school and almost twenty-four years old, that respect for your teachers doesn't come as easily as it did when you were sixteen and naive. You begin to look at things differently, the teacher needed to start earning your respect. And for the first time, you start to wonder why your teachers aren't respecting you in return.

"I'll be in touch," he stood up and held out his hand. I couldn't read the expression on his face. I had no idea if I had impressed him or been an utter disappointment.

"I hope to hear from you soon," I shook his hand. He gave me a tight-lipped smile and I let myself out.

As I exited the building, I turned my phone back on and was happy to see that the vibrating sound from earlier had been a text message from Hayden confirming our date for Saturday night. I felt an energetic rush when reading his message. Even though bowling wasn't exactly my idea of a rocking Saturday night, I was more than willing to go out with Hayden again. I quickly replied and asked him if it was indeed Bowlmor in Union Square that he was referring to. He wrote back yes, confirming my suspicions. I instantly had a flash-back to my eleventh birthday party where I rolled nothing but gutter balls because my parents told me I was too old to use the bumper lanes. This was different, though. Something told me he wouldn't laugh at me if I bowled terribly. So I bit the bullet and told him I'd love to go.

Heading toward Jane Street, I scrolled through my text messages and emails to see if I had anything from Cassandra. There was nothing. I was still reeling from the way she acted at lunch, so callous and aloof. Like our entire friendship was just an afterthought to her. I didn't want to let it slide, though, we had to talk it out. I opened my text messages on my phone and decided to compose a message.

Hey, Cassandra. I think we need to chat. Call me when you get a chance.

I hit send just as I rounded the corner and saw Michael waiting for me outside the coffee shop. He was talking to someone on the phone. I walked a little slower so I wouldn't interrupt him, but as soon as he saw me he rushed off the phone and shoved it into his back pocket.

"Hey there," my heart rate picked up slightly as he moved closer. I swallowed hard and nervously folded my arms.

"How did it go?" he asked, holding the door open for me.

"I'm not exactly sure. Dr. Greenfield is a tough man to read. He sure did make me nervous, though."

"I'm sure you did fine," he said in a reassuring tone.

We ordered our coffees, mine a soy latte, his black, and sat down on an old, beat-up couch in the middle of the joint. The place was crowded and loud, like most coffee shops in the Village. I sipped my latte and let Dr. Greenfield's words wash over me. What did I want to do when I finished at NYU?

"Do you have any big plans this weekend?" Michael asked, studying his coffee cup.

"I'm actually going out with that guy Hayden again," I studied Michael's face for the faintest hint of a reaction. His face remained unreadable. "What about you?"

Michael paused and took a sip of his coffee. I still wondered how he drank it black.

"I'm going to be spending most of the day Saturday doing work, and then Sunday I might be getting brunch with Angela by where she lives in Brooklyn Heights."

"So the two of you are dating," I said, not as much as a question but more as a statement.

"I'm not sure," he offered. He looked at me and opened his mouth to say something, but then pressed his lips into a tight smile. "Is it okay that I'm talking to you about this? I mean, is it weird?"

Of course it was weird. Just a few months ago I was madly in love with Michael. But in all fairness I had told him about Hayden, so I guess it was my turn to feel uncomfortable.

"No," I lied. "It's perfectly fine. I mean, we're friends. Right?" I reached over and grabbed his coffee, taking a sip.

"Good?" he teased.

"I don't know how you drink this stuff?" I grimaced.

He took the coffee cup out of my hands and placed it on the wobbly table beside him. "I guess we are," he smiled. "Friends, that is. We were once before."

"It might get a little awkward, though. I have seen you naked."

Michael let out a low, breathy laugh, slightly choking on his coffee. "That's true you have. But I won't let it get in the way, if you won't."

"Agreed," I laughed. "So, then, come on. Tell me about Angela. Or Angie as Olivia likes to call her."

"Alright fine. She's a fun girl," he admitted. "I like her, from what I've seen of her so far." He stopped to take another sip of his coffee. "She does give me the run-around a lot, though."

"How do you mean?"

"Well, I'll ask her to hang out, and she is usually always busy doing something else, or she says she'll let me know. Very non-committal. I can't really blame her. We're all busy with school, but I'm always the one initiating things with her. I do like her, though."

I couldn't help but laugh. Michael had found the female version of himself. It was poetic justice.

"So you're chasing this girl? She's got you hooked."

"I wouldn't say that," he said in a mock-defensive tone. "But I do like her. I just can't tell if she likes me back."

"But you're going to keep trying?" I ask with a sarcastic grin.

"Yes, I am. And what is with this big smile on your face?"

"I just don't understand why you would waste your time with this girl!"

"I don't know," he laughed. "I told you, I like her."

I leaned in a little closer to Michael and looked in his big, gorgeous brown eyes. Commanding myself not to melt right then and there, I stayed on topic.

"Do you think it's possible that the only reason you're so into this girl is because you can't tell if she's into you back?" I put it as simply as possible.

"What are you talking about?" he asked, seemingly genuinely interested in my opinion.

"You really want to know?"

He nodded, reaching over for his coffee, spilling a little for good measure. He was now grasping his mug with both hands.

"The thing of it is, girls don't usually like to play games," I declared. "At least not with guys they really like."

Michael leaned back and seemed to consider this for a moment. "Go on."

"It's the same thing as a guy," I continued. "If he really likes you, he's going to ask you out. He's not going to give you the run-around and make you sit and wonder why he hasn't called. So if Angela really wants to make time for you, then she'll do it." I shook my head and laughed. "But for some reason you all seem to love it. You guys love the hunt."

Michael raised both of his eyebrows. "The hunt?"

"Yes," I threw my hands in the air. "You know what I mean. The hunt, the chase, whatever you want to call it. If you really like this girl, and you want it to go somewhere, your best option is to talk to her about why she keeps blowing you off. If she gives you double talk, or is evasive, then you have your answer."

"And if she doesn't give me double talk?" he asked with a smirk.

"If she proves you wrong?"

"Then you found someone who can talk openly about their feelings," I tucked a strand of hair behind my ear and shrugged. "And if that's the case, you're one of the lucky ones."

It felt strange giving Michael relationship advice. Just a year ago I would have been going crazy at the mere mention of him being interested in another girl. But somehow dating Hayden made it easier. More tolerable.

Michael shook his coffee cup, indicating that it was empty and let out a sigh.

"We should do this more often," he said. "Not just you and me, but all of us. Let's all get a drink next week after class, like we used to."

"I think that can be arranged," I said. It felt good to have Michael back in my life. I really had missed talking to him. "And in light of us agreeing to be friends again, there's something I want to tell you. About a month ago, right when I got back from Brazil, I ran into Marge."

The blood drained from Michael's face and his eyes went wide. "You ran into Marge? As in, my ex-girlfriend?"

I nodded. "She sort of came up to me in the street," I said calmly. "And slapped me across the face."

Michael's mouth hung open and he swiftly placed his hand over it.

"You're not serious, are you?" he asked with a breathy voice. "She slapped you? That's insane, how did she even know who you were?"

"I have no idea!" I let out a soft chuckle. "I was walking with Olivia and she pretty much charged at me from down the street, asked me if my name was Amalia, and then slapped me right there!"

"I am so sorry," he said. Only he didn't look sorry, he was laughing.

"Are you honestly laughing about this?" I swatted his arm. "That girl is nuts. I can't believe you dated her!"

"I don't mean to laugh," he wiped under his eyes. "But it's just so ludicrous." He shook his head and then a flicker of recognition flashed across his face. "My sister must have told her about you."

"Your sister?"

"Yeah," he started to explain. "She and Marge were friendly. When my sister, Amanda, asked me why Marge and I broke up, I told her about you."

I raised an eyebrow. "What exactly did you tell her?"

"Not the entire story," he quickly jumped in. "An abridged version. But obviously she thought Marge had the right to know. And considering we live in a post-Facebook world, I'm sure she looked you up to see what you looked like."

"Well, mystery solved." I rubbed my forehead.

He shrugged and shook his head. "I really am sorry she slapped you. I honestly don't even speak to her anymore."

"It's over and done with. I'm just glad she didn't punch me," I said. "Besides, I kind of deserved it."

Michael moved closer to me on the couch and covered my hands with his. "No you didn't," he had a surprised look on his face. "Why would you say that?"

When he touched me, I felt the familiar mixture of overpowering feelings that used to occur. I looked down and carefully moved my hand away, willing my heart rate to return to normal.

"I slept with her boyfriend," I said with a grimace. "If I had found out Nicholas cheated on me, I may have done the same thing. Actually, no, scratch that. I would have slapped him in the face, not her."

"Exactly. If anyone deserved a slap in that situation, it was me," he nodded.

"Now that I can agree on," I grinned. I took my coffee mug and softly tapped it against his.

"See, this friend stuff is working out already," he said. "We should have done this weeks ago."

"Absolutely," I said in agreement. I took the last remaining sip of my coffee and smiled. "What could possibly go wrong?"

Chapter 20

Olivia

"Okay, that is officially the third thing I've tripped over!" Stumbling to regain my balance, I bent down to pick up a random high-heeled shoe and held it up in the air. "Seriously, Amalia, when are you going to unpack? You've been here for weeks!"

"Um," she peered around her apartment and softly touched her pointer finger to her lip. I raised an eyebrow to prompt her to answer me. She laughed and gave me a wide, fake smile. "Tomorrow?" She had just gotten out of the shower and was wearing an over-sized baby-blue robe and fuzzy slippers. I was honestly surprised that she was able to find so much as a towel in the essential squalor she was living in. Not because the apartment was in bad shape, far from it, but because there were boxes and clothes everywhere. Her new place was smaller than the last one, only a one-bedroom, which made more sense since she was living by herself. Her bedroom was very small, barely fitting a full-sized bed. The counter tops in the cooking area were made out of the same fake granite we saw in the apartment-from-hell last month, but these were in much better shape. There was a small, electric stove top and a mid-sized refrigerator. There wasn't really enough room for a table of any kind, so she'd have to do what most city-dwellers did and put stools to sit at the edge of her counter top.

The floors were laminate instead of hardwood like in her former apartment, but they looked pretty real to the untrained eye. All in all, a decent apartment for the $1,900 dollars a month she was spending (plus utilities, of course). I still wasn't sure how she managed to cough up the money to pay for the security deposit, but I didn't want to make her feel uncomfortable and pry.

"Come on, Olivia, I need your help!" she stood with her hands on her hips. "What does a person wear to go bowling?"

"Jeans and a T-Shirt?" I offered. "Oh, and don't forget to bring socks in case you have to put on bowling shoes!"

She walked back into the bathroom and retrieved a large paddle hairbrush. She then spun out of the bathroom and held the brush under her chin, pretending it was a microphone and she was hosting a talk show. She pointed it at me and smiled. "You're a genius," she declared, and danced back into the bathroom.

"I know," I called to her as I sat down on her bed. There was a pile of clothes at the foot of the bed. I couldn't tell if they had been recently washed or not. I looked around her new place some more. It was the first time she had let me inside since she moved in and now I understood why. "You know this bed is the only seat in your apartment?"

"That's because most of the furniture in my old apartment was Christina's," she came back out, dressed this time. She had on tight, skinny jeans, and a flowy three-quarter-sleeved top. It was more of a dressed-up version of jeans and a T-shirt, but she still looked good in it. She took a look around, scanning the entire apartment and grimaced. "I think I need to take a trip to Ikea."

"Ikea?" I scoffed.

"You don't think I'd rather be making a day of it at Restoration Hardware? Ikea is about all I can afford right now. Maybe a few end tables from Target," she flipped her head over and brushed her long, curly hair out. "I think I am going to blow out my hair tonight, make it straight." She grabbed a pair of socks from a box marked "clothes" and sniffed them to make sure they were clean.

142

"Hayden's never seen it straight before." She smiled the whole time she spoke to me.

"You really like him, don't you?" I hadn't seen her smile this much the entire time I'd known her. It felt like she was really over Michael, or at least over him enough to give Hayden a real chance.

"I do," the smile remained on her lips. She couldn't even hide it. She was glowing. "And I owe you to thank. All because you made me invite him out that night."

Amalia headed back into the bathroom to finish getting ready and I followed her. Even though she was glowing at the mere mention of Hayden's name, I still had to ask if she had another guy on her mind.

"Do you still have feelings for Michael at all?" I blurted out. I knew this would catch her off guard, but I was genuinely curious. "You ended up grabbing coffee with him the other day after class, right?"

She picked up a tube of lipstick and studied it. She twirled it around in her fingers a few times before finally answering me.

"Yeah, we got coffee. And I honestly don't know how I feel," she admitted. The smile left her face and was replaced with a look of discomfort. She walked over to me and plopped down on the bed. "When I'm with Hayden. It feels so comfortable. I feel like I can really be myself around him. And there's no wondering how he feels about me because he's completely honest about his feelings. I mean look at me, I can't stop smiling!"

"But?" I prompted.

She let out a deep sigh. "But when I'm with Michael, I feel like everything inside me comes alive," she said with wide eyes. "But it's all wrapped up in all of this uncertainty and evasiveness. I *never* know what he's thinking. I don't even know if he still looks at me that way. We actually discussed trying to be friends." She pushed herself off the bed and reached for her make-up bag. She examined each tool as she took them out one by one.

I flashed back to my meeting with Nate on the subway. I hadn't thought about him since that night I ran into him, but something about the way Amalia described Michael resonated with me. Memories of Nate and me desperately kissing, unable to get enough of each other. Of me sneaking him into my house late at night, when my parents told me I wasn't allowed to see him anymore. The strongest were the memories of us making love in his car. We always thought it was more fun to risk getting caught then to go at it in my dorm room. It was more romantic that way. More intense. I wanted to tell her that I understood what she was going through. That I knew what it was like to be driven to someone by pure passion. But I decided this wasn't the time.

"He still looks at you that way," I uttered. "I catch him glaring at you constantly."

She grimaced. "He's probably just checking out my ass."

I laughed and shook my head. "Look, I'm not trying to upset you, but do you really think you can just be friends?" I asked with genuine concern. "Won't it hurt you?"

"I have no idea," she admitted. She picked up a blush brush, studied it, and put it back down. Her shoulders deflated and she rubbed her temples. "But I don't want to think about it right now. Tonight is my date with Hayden." She shook her head and stood up a little straighter. "Handsome, sweet, well-mannered Hayden. Who I can't wait to go out with, so no more talk about Michael."

"I got it," I put up my hands. "I'm sorry I brought it up."

"Don't worry about it. Seriously. You're the only person who I can talk to about how this all makes me feel," she switched her weight from one foot to another. "God knows, Cassandra's not one for hanging out these days. She never got in touch with me after that lunch from hell we had. I even called Aaron to see if he could give me an insight as to why she's been acting so weird, but he didn't have anything for me."

"Why would Aaron know?" I asked.

"Well because they were both here this summer, and I thought they were going to spend all this time together. But apparently she

144

blew him off every chance she got."

"Have you seen Aaron since you've been home?" I asked.

"No," she shook her head. "But he's going to come in to the city for my birthday. It would be nice if we all could do something fun. Cassie included."

"I don't understand what's going on with her," I plucked some of Amalia's clothes off the floor and began to fold them. I didn't know Cassandra too well. I had met her last year through Amalia. Before she started acting so strangely, she always seemed fun to be around. "But still, I'm sorry if I upset you at all with the Michael comment."

"Really, it's fine." She motioned for me to follow her into the bathroom again. "But if you truly feel that bad about it, you can make it up to me by straightening my hair for me." She gave me an over-the-top smile.

"No problem," I laughed. "Now if we could just find the straightening iron in this mess!"

Chapter 21

Amalia

After a quick impromptu elevator ride Hayden and I arrived on the top floor of Bowlmor. It was 8:30 on a Saturday night and although the bowling alley was busy, Hayden had reserved a lane for the two of us and we were shown to it right away. The entire place was literally glowing; it felt like something out of an 80's movies, only with current top-40 music playing. The lanes were shining with colored lights that kept changing from blue to purple. Even the bowling balls were bright neon colors. After exchanging our shoes for the more embarrassing, yet required, footwear we entered our names into computer-type gadget and a waitress immediately materialized to take our drink order.

"I'll have a Mojito," I ordered, while testing out some of the bowling-ball choices. I wanted to find the lightest one possible to lower the risk of my injuring, or more likely, embarrassing myself.

"That sounds good," Hayden said with a nod. "I'll have the same."

Hayden walked behind me and slid his arms around my waist. "Let me guess," he said with a grin. "You're going to pick that pink ball right there."

I turned around to face him. He was much taller than me, nearly a foot. I stood on my toes and gently pressed my lips against his.

"And so what if I do?" I said in a mocking tone. "Maybe I like pink!" Or maybe the ball was only eight pounds and I didn't feel like straining myself.

"Well maybe I like pink too," he effortlessly picked up the bowling ball with one hand. "Maybe this should be my ball for the evening."

"I'll flip you for it," I said with a straight face. "Heads, the ball's mine."

Hayden laughed and leaned in for another kiss. "It's all yours, beautiful."

I smiled triumphantly and took what was rightfully mine. "Let's get this over with," I uttered.

"Not a fan of bowling?" he said, retrieving a heavier, neon-blue ball from the rack. The waitress came back around with our cocktails and softly placed them down on the small table by our lane, careful not to spill any.

"No it's not that," I made my way up to the lane, holding the pink ball in both arms. "Just not very good at it." I stopped behind the black line and let the person next to me bowl first. It was something I was taught when I was a child. Bowling etiquette. When the guy next to me was finished, I slipped my fingers into the three holes in the ball. I looked straight ahead at the ten, neatly stacked pins, and positioned myself in the center of the lane.

"You can do it!" Hayden called out to me.

Nervously, I pulled my right arm back, gripping the inside of the ball with my fingertips. I could touch the inside of the ball with my nails. It was an unpleasant feeling. With one forceful thrust, I rolled the ball down the alley. Despite all of the energy I put behind it, the ball moved slowly toward the pins. I didn't even think it would make it all the way to the end of the lane, but it did. To my surprise, the ball collided with the pins, effortlessly knocking eight of them down. My eyes widened in shock, but I didn't let Hayden see.

"I thought you said you weren't good at this?" Hayden folded his arms across his chest in mock annoyance. He raised his eyebrows, waiting for an explanation.

I walked back toward him and took a sip of my drink. "I guess I'm better than I remembered." I did an over-the-top hair flip and shot him a wink.

My ball came back around and the machine spit it out onto the belt. I picked it back up and made my way back to the lane. In one smooth roll, I managed to knock over the two remaining pins. I couldn't believe it; I wasn't actually half bad. I turned back to Hayden, whose hands were now on his hips.

"Are you trying to swindle me?" he joked. He typed my score into the computer and then lightly jogged over to where I was.

"I would never do such a thing!" I put my hand on my chest and pretended to gasp.

Hayden took my hand and walked me over to the chairs by the table with our drinks on it. He sat me down and smiled.

"What are you smiling at?" I asked, grinning like a fool myself.

"I like your hair like this," he twisted a strand of blonde between his fingers. "I like it curly too, though."

"Thank you," I smiled. "I was trying something new."

"Just for me?" he asked with a hopeful look in his eye.

I nodded.

"I really like spending time with you, Amalia," he lifted my chin with the tip of his finger and lightly kissed me. Goosebumps shot up and down my arms as I leaned into his soft lips. "Would you want to stay the night at my apartment?"

"Tonight?" I asked, leaning back in my chair.

"Yes," he muttered softly in my ear. "Tonight."

I couldn't stop myself from saying yes. Hayden bit his bottom lip and I felt a rush of excitement wash over me.

"I'll stay with you tonight," I said, standing back up. "But first, I think I'll finish kicking your ass at bowling."

Chapter 22

Olivia

Monday morning I was enjoying a peaceful, solitary moment sitting on a bench in Washington Square Park, when I saw Amalia power-walking over to me. Her blonde curls bounced around her, as if independent from her body, as she picked up the pace.

"Hey," I said, moving over a bit to make room for her on the bench. "What's going on?"

"I had a feeling you'd be here," she said with a huge grin on her face. "I have to tell you something."

"Okay?" I laughed at her joker-sized grinned. "What is it?"

She looked back and forth, as if this was top-secret information. "I slept with Hayden after our date." She clapped her hands together and let out a small laugh. The girl was downright giddy.

"Finally!" I said.

"What do you mean finally?" her voice growing louder. "We only went out on one date."

"Maybe officially," I offered. "But the two of you have been playing cat and mouse with each other since last year. I'm just saying, it's about time."

"Uh huh," she reached down and took a sip from a Starbucks cup I just noticed she was carrying.

"Are you ever without coffee?" I asked.

"What kind of question is that?" she shook her head.

"Alright, so back to the event," I said. "How was it?"

She smiled with the straw still in her mouth. "It was wonderful."

"Wow, really?"

"It was soft and sweet, kind of like you see in the movies. I felt really safe," she said. "Not that I usually feel unsafe when sleeping with guys. But he definitely went out of his way to make me happy. He didn't make me feel like it was all about him, like so many guys do."

"Tell me about it," I nodded. I had certainly been with my share of that type of guy. Luckily, Alex always made me feel safe and loved. "I'm really happy for you, Amalia. I think you found one of the good ones."

She just smiled and bounced around a bit more on the bench. I hoped this encounter finally meant Michael had been exorcized from her system. But something told me it wasn't going to be that easy.

A few weeks had passed and just as Dr. Greenfield was packing up the end of class for the day, he mournfully reported that our grades for our first exam would be posted outside in the hallway. Apparently, a few people didn't do so well. After tracking down the chart and waiting in line to be able to view it, I slid my finger along where my student number was and followed it all the way to my grade. A-.

"Alright!" I said. Alex was behind me and gave me a little squeeze. Then I stepped to the side, letting him stand in front of me to check his own score. He too slid his finger across the large paper posted on the wall. I couldn't help but glance over his shoulder. To my delight, he received the same grade as me. He turned around and rewarded me with another hug, this time lifting my entire body off the floor. A few of the other students let out grunts, as they looked over their grades. A few others shook their heads at us for being so inappropriate. "This school has a giant stick up its ass," I mumbled.

"Tell me about it," he nodded in agreement. He looked around for a moment and then whispered in my ear. "I wish I knew Michael's student code so I could check his grade."

We made a beeline for the exit, our good grades making us anxious to get out of the building.

"The two of you have always been in silent competition with each other, haven't you?" I asked, giving him the side-eye.

Alex just gave me a loaded look, confirming my suspicions.

"Don't even think about him," I squeezed his hand twice. "You'll get in no matter what!"

"Get into what?" he asked.

"To whatever doctoral program you apply to get into when we graduate," I said with a smile. "What, you don't think you will?"

"Oh no, I know I will."

"There's the cocky boy I know and love," I laughed.

"And what about you?" he asked. "Which programs will you be applying to? There are a lot of great doctoral programs right here in New York."

"I haven't decided yet," I dodged the question. Graduate school at NYU was stressful enough without having the added pressure of worrying about applying to another school next year. If I wanted to pursue my doctorate, I could always try to stay at NYU. Although, that wouldn't be as easy as it sounded. I heard that last semester they only accepted nine people into the program I'd be applying for. Alex, as a man, already had an unfair advantage. Most of the students in my program were female. I shook my head, trying to rid myself of these negative thoughts and reached for his hand. "Now come on, we have to get to Bloomingdales before it gets insanely crowded."

"Why exactly do I need to accompany you on this trip?" he said in a faux sarcastic tone.

I looked around the street to make sure there weren't too many people around. When I knew the coast was clear, I stood up on

153

my toes, craned my neck, and kissed him. First sweet and softly, then harder, with more passion. I pulled away just as I could tell he was getting into it, and gave him an innocent grin.

"Because we need to pick out a present for Amalia's birthday next week," I replied, still grinning triumphantly. "Don't forget, we're all getting drinks together. Like we used to."

"You're very manipulative," he raised both eyebrows. Then pulled me in for another kiss.

I gently swatted him off. "Come on, we have to go!"

"As you wish, princess."

"Oh, very funny," I grimaced. Just then my phone started to buzz. I reached for it from my purse, expecting it to be either Amalia or Angela.

But it wasn't. It was Nate.

Alex reached over and took the still-vibrating phone out of my hands. As quickly as the smile had appeared on his face, it washed away. "Is this who I think it is? Why is your ex-boyfriend calling you?"

I froze, unable to speak. I never told Alex that I ran into Nate. It seemed harmless at the time, honestly it still did. But now here it was, glowing on my phone. Something I had hidden. Even though it wasn't a big deal, it was going to seem like one now.

"He shouldn't even still be in New York," I mumbled under my breath.

"What did you say?" Alex raised his eyebrows.

The phone vibrated one more time and Alex raised his hand to answer it.

"Don't," I said in a stern voice. "Just ignore it."

Alex's mouth was pressed into a tight, straight line. He repeated his question, slower this time. "Why is your ex-boyfriend calling you?"

I couldn't really blame him for being angry. As far as he knew, Nate and I hadn't spoken since college. I always said you couldn't be friends with an ex, it just caused problems. These were clearly

154

the problems I was referring to.

"I don't know,' I answered softly.

The phone stopped vibrating and Alex handed it back to me, scowling at it like it was a dirty bag of garbage.

I gingerly removed it from his hands and tucked it back into my purse, the whole time thinking of what to say to him. I figured I might as well go with the truth. I really hadn't done anything wrong.

"Look," I started speaking in a rapid tone. "I ran into him a few weeks ago the night I came looking for you. He was waiting on the train platform and we talked for all of five minutes. I haven't seen or heard from him since."

"So then why is he calling you now?" Alex glared at me. "And why didn't you just tell me you ran into him if it was so harmless. Do you still have feelings for him?"

I winced at his accusation, but I wasn't sure why. "I have no idea why he's calling me now! And I didn't tell you because it was nothing."

"You didn't answer the most important question, Olivia," he took a step toward me. He spoke in a calm, measured voice, but I could tell even talking about this was extremely upsetting to him. He took a deep breath and asked me again, more softly this time. "Do you still have feelings for him?"

I paused. Just for a moment, but there it was. A pause long enough to confirm doubt. Long enough to make Alex question my true feelings for him. A pause long enough to make me question if just maybe he was right. I wanted to say something to him. Something comforting and reassuring, but I was too shocked to speak. For a brief moment I thought I saw tears in his eyes, but he reached for his aviator sunglasses so quickly I couldn't really tell. We both stood in silence for a moment until Alex finally spoke, saying the last thing I could possibly want to hear.

"Listen, Olivia," he began, his painful serenade through a cracking voice. "I think we should spend some time apart."

And there it was. The kind of words that echo through you, that make you wish you could turn back time and relive the seconds right before. Make that last kiss last just a few moment longer, the last hug just a few beats tighter. My lips started to quiver and I glanced down at my hands, which had been shaking since this conversation began. He didn't say anything else and neither did I. I opened my mouth to speak, but couldn't make a sound. So instead of staying, he just lit up a cigarette, turned on his heel, and walked into the crowd. Within seconds he was no longer visible; Manhattan had swallowed him whole. Long, hot streams flowed down my cheeks, landing on my lips, on my clothes, in my hair. I didn't have the energy to wipe them off.

I stood a little longer. I was not exactly sure how much time had passed. Minutes, maybe half an hour. I pulled a pocket mirror out of my purse and did my best to fix my face. I switched the mirror out of my cigarettes, and lit one up. Savoring the sting, followed by the sweet relaxation it quickly offered in return. There was no way I was making it to Bloomingdales this afternoon. Amalia could do with a gift card, I resolved. I pulled out my own over-sized Michael Kors sunglasses to cover up my puffy face and numbly made my way home.

Chapter 23

Amalia

"I don't know what happened between them," I paused to sip my birthday cosmopolitan. "She hasn't told me much, and it does seem really out of nowhere. I don't even think they've spoken since they broke up."

"It's just a little odd," Hayden nodded. "From what you've told me, Olivia and Alex seemed like the perfect couple. Why would they just break up out of the blue like that?"

"Beats me!" I shrugged. "Maybe I can try to get some information out of her after she's had a few drinks.

A few weeks after Olivia and Alex's unexpected uncoupling, Hayden and I were sitting up at the bar at a local watering hole called the High Point. I had never been there before, but a few of the other students frequented this place, and I figured it was low-key enough to have a few birthday drinks. After all, anything would be better than the surprise party from hell that Cassandra threw for me last year. It was sheer luck that my birthday happened to fall on a Friday this year, and everyone who I invited out said they could make it. Which to my amazement, included Cassie. It was a relatively nice night for October, the bitter wind seemed to hold off just long enough so I could enjoy turning 24. It was now 9 pm, about half an hour before everyone else was supposed to arrive. Hayden wanted to buy me my first drink of the night and insisted on it being a Cosmopolitan. He hadn't ordered anything himself yet; he just sat and watched as I struggled with my pinkish-red cocktail.

"Why am I drinking this again?" I twirled the stem of a maraschino cherry that I had already eaten around in my drink. Over the small crowd I could hear "1979" by the Smashing Pumpkins playing in the background.

"I saw it on an episode of *Sex and the City* once," he shrugged. "I thought you might like it. Plus it's magenta-colored and there's even an orange wedge. It looks festive."

"Just once, though, right?" I lightly teased. "You only watched *Sex and the City* once?"

"I'll let you tease me, because it's your birthday."

"I love the show, the drink, however, is not really my taste," I grimaced.

"Let me have a sip," he plucked the glass from my hand. "How bad can it be?"

"Brace yourself, partner."

Hayden slowly sipped the liquid and immediately recoiled in disgust. "Oh my God, it tastes like a Rainbow Brite doll!"

I gave him an all-knowing grin and motioned for the bartender. "Jack and ginger, please." The bartender nodded and turned to Hayden.

"Bourbon," he coughed, sliding the Cosmo back to the bartender. "Straight."

I patted him on the back and pretended to console him. He regained his composure and pulled me in for a kiss. I kissed him back, but then playfully pushed him off.

"No kissing, you have Cosmo-breath!" I joked.

"Fine, no kissing," he said, pretending to be offended. Then he reached into his coat pocket and pulled out a small, rectangular box wrapped neatly with pink and gold wrapping paper. "Can it be time for presents instead?"

159

For a moment, my heart stopped. I swear, just one beat missed. Time stood still for one, entire, second. I don't know why I felt nervous. From the shape of the box I could tell it wasn't anything to sweat over. It wasn't an engagement ring. But still, I felt my stomach drop. Hayden and I hadn't even had the conversation about being exclusive and here before me sat a gift that was, by the looks of it, either a bracelet or a necklace. The fact of the matter was, no man had ever bought jewelry for me before, apart from my dad when I was a child. I gingerly took the perfectly wrapped gift from Hayden's hand and stared at it.

"Well, go on," he smiled eagerly. "Open it."

I smiled politely and gently tugged at the shimmering paper, wondering if he had got it at Papyrus. Underneath the wrapping was a dark-blue box with the word Swarovski imprinted on it. As I opened the box, I felt my heart race a little faster, but still couldn't pinpoint why. Inside lay a beautiful silver bracelet with pale-blue crystals dangling off the sides. I usually didn't like anything that resembled a charm bracelet, but this was different. This was perfect. I felt my eyes well up with tears, touched by Hayden's gesture. I kept my head down for an extra moment and blinked them back so he couldn't tell I was getting too emotional. I simply smiled and told him it was beautiful.

"Just like you," he replied. "Can I put it on you?"

I nodded.

Hayden carefully removed the bracelet from its box and fastened it to my right wrist. It looked even better on my arm than in the box.

"Thank you so much," I touched his cheek. "It's lovely."

He smiled and reached for my hand. Picking it up to his lips, he softly kissed it. "Amalia, there's something I want to talk to you about. Before your friends show up."

"What is it?" I asked timidly.

"I don't know how to ask this without sounding like an eighth-grader," he said with a soft laugh. His lips were pulled into a straight line, and his eyes were wide with anticipation. "Will you be my girlfriend?"

I didn't respond.

"I know," he looked down at his drink. "Utterly corny."

"No," I said quietly, reaching for his hand. I didn't know what to say except, "It's not corny at all."

"I want to be with you, and only you. I feel like we just click. It's so easy when I am with you. There's no hyped-up drama, or anxiety-induced panic over the next time you're going to return my call. I look forward to seeing you every time we make plans, and I find myself wishing you were around more often when we aren't together. What I am trying to say here is, I want to date only you. Exclusively."

It was beautiful. It was direct, it was romantic, and, most importantly, it was honest. But I still couldn't say yes. A part of me still wasn't ready to be in a relationship. I didn't know if it was what Nicholas put me through, or Michael, or both. But I found myself saying no to this proposition and hoping that he would still want to continue to see me until I was ready for more. Until I was ready to fully commit.

"I don't want to stop seeing you," I said in an attempt to salvage us. "I'm just not ready for that kind of commitment. It doesn't mean I won't be in the future, I'm just not there right now."

"I had a feeling you'd say that," Hayden replied, offering me a kind smile. "And it's alright."

"It is?" I breathed a sigh of relief.

"It is. I'll wait until you're ready," he said. "Just know that I'm not seeing anyone but you."

"You really are a great guy, you know that?"

"And you're a great girl," he replied. "Which is why I will wait."

We looked at each other for a moment, both unsure of our next move. I heard footsteps behind me and realized that someone from my group had arrived. I felt relieved that Olivia had shown up just in time to break the tension.

"Hey guys," she said, looking downcast. She was slightly more dressed-up than usual, wearing a collared blouse with a dark-purple cardigan over it, dark-wash skinny jeans, and for once three-inch heels. Her brown hair flowed with soft waves and her lipstick was bright, movie-star red.

"Olivia, you look gorgeous!" I stood to give her a hug. "How are you feeling?"

"Awful," she replied with no apprehension. She scanned the bar for a moment and sighed. "Is Alex coming here tonight?"

Hayden and I looked at each other, unsure of what to say.

"No, sweetie. I don't think he is," I shook my head.

"That's fine," she said through a fake smile. "I didn't expect him to come anyway."

"Do you think you and I could have some time to talk later?" I asked her. "Just you and me?" I was so curious to know what would prompt Alex to break up with her so coldly. There had to be more to the story she wasn't telling me.

"Of course," she said, giving me the best smile she could muster up. "It's your birthday; you get whatever you want."

"That's true," I laughed. Hayden nodded in agreement.

"Speaking of which!" a genuine smile returned to her face as she rummaged through her purse. "I have something for you."

She pulled out a tiny pink tiara with the number 24 on it and playfully showed it off to me.

"What the hell is that?" I asked, fearing I already knew the answer.

"It's your birthday crown," she said in a declarative tone.

I looked at Hayden for help, but he gave me a glance that suggested I do what she wanted or she might start crying.

"Awesome, Olivia. I love it," I bent down so she could place the teeny crown on top of my head. I felt the small combs push into my curls, ripping out some of my hair in the process. "Thank you so much. Now everyone in the bar will know it's my birthday." I gritted my teeth and could just barely hear Hayden snickering behind me.

"Well, now, that that's settled you can tell me who else is coming tonight!" she laughed. "Also, I could use a drink."

I waved to the bartender to come and take her drink order. Rum and coke, as usual.

"I invited Cassandra, who, believe it or not, actually promised to show up," I said as I reclaimed my seat at the bar. The place was starting to fill out, and I certainly didn't want to spend the entire night standing in my high heels. "I also invited Aaron, who should be here any minute!"

"Your brother's coming?" she asked, sounding surprised.

"He is!" I grinned. "I'm very excited about it. I haven't seen him in months!"

I heard a vibration on the bar and noticed it was Hayden's cell going off.

"I'm going to let you two chat for a moment," Hayden stood up. "I just got a call from work and I hate to do this but I have to take it. I'll be gone ten minutes tops, I promise." He offered his stool to Olivia, who happily took it.

"I'll start the stopwatch," I said, pointing to the clock in the corner.

As soon as Hayden walked out the front door, Olivia leaned in closer to me. "Did you invite Michael?"

"I did," I answered, suddenly feeling guilty about it. Hayden didn't exactly know the entire story about Michael and me. All he knew was that he was a classmate. A lie of omission.

"Wow. That might get a little awkward," she said.

"Oh please," I fiddled with the tiara that was destroying my hair. "If he even shows up."

"You have a point," Olivia said, as the bartender handed her a drink. "I wonder if he'll bring Angela."

"I guess he can if he wants to. We are trying to be friends," I slightly stumbled over the word.

Olivia just shook her head and sipped her cocktail. "I'm worried this isn't a good idea for you."

"You know, there's something else *I* am wondering about," I said, thinking now was as good a time as ever to ask her what was really on my mind. "What exactly happened between you and Alex? Did you really just break up over Nate calling you? It seems a little extreme."

Olivia took a deep breath, shook her head again, and took an even longer sip of her rum and coke.

"No, it's not that simple. You don't know the whole story," she said, her eyes fixed on her drink. "About me in college. About Nate and me."

"No, I don't really know anything about him," I shrugged. "I just know he was your college boyfriend."

"He was the love of my life," she spat out. "Or at least I thought he was." She lowered her eyes to the ground.

I nodded and motioned for her to go on with her story.

"When we met, we were both interning at the same hospital. We were both single at the time, and there was an instant connection, but there was also a strict no-fraternizing policy among co-workers."

"So what happened?" I asked, confused and intrigued by her story.

"We didn't care," she uttered. "And ultimately it cost me my internship."

"Your supervisor found out?"

"She did," Olivia said. "Not only that, but when my parents asked me why I got the boot, I told them the truth. Ever since then, they've hated Nate. They told me he wasn't allowed in our house during Christmas or Spring Break, and they even threatened to stop paying my tuition if I continued to see him."

"Oh my God," I replied. "How did I not know any of this?"

"Because I don't like to talk about it," she admitted. "But the reason Alex doesn't like him is because when we first started dating, I told him how passionate I had been about Nate. The notion of us not being allowed to date, either at work or because

164

of my family, was intoxicating. I made a lot of bad decisions, and finally, after a couple of years, I called it off." She ran her fingers over her cardigan, fidgeting with the buttons. "The ugly truth was that he didn't really care about me. He had a wandering eye and even though we were exclusive, I never felt like he was truly committed to the relationship. On top of all that he never wanted to leave Florida and I knew I was going to go to graduate school in New York. I may have finally got the courage to break it off, but it destroyed me. Alex knows all of this, and that's why he got so angry when he saw Nate calling. Also, because I had run into him a week prior and never told him."

I raised an eyebrow. I couldn't believe that Olivia, being so straight-laced, could have such a sordid tale to tell.

"When did you run into him?"

"It was the night of that party for Cassandra's boss," she explained. "He was on the same subway platform as me. He told me he was in town on vacation. I spoke to him for literally five minutes."

"Why didn't you just tell Alex this?"

"I don't know!" she threw her hands in the air. "I saw Nate, and it just did something to me. All logic went out the window. I'm not in love with him anymore... but just seeing him again made me feel a bit crazy."

"It sounds like your relationship was very difficult," I offered. "I am so sorry you had to go through any of that."

"I realize now, looking back on it, that I wasn't in love with him. That I was attracted to the drama. It made every moment together so passionate. But it wasn't real." She looked like she might start to cry again, and I put a hand on her shoulder. "I'm not even attracted to Nate now. What I had with Alex, that was real. And I sabotaged it."

"You need to tell him this," I said. "Maybe you two can get back together"

She nodded. "Yeah, maybe."

Hayden came back just as Olivia was finishing up her story. She quickly wiped her face and went to stand up, but he told her to remain seated. He would stand for the night.

"Sorry about that, ladies," he said. "Amalia, I ran into your brother outside. And I think Cassandra too." Hayden hadn't met my brother before, but I had shown him enough pictures of us on Facebook for him to recognize Aaron right away.

"Yeah?" I said, perking up.

"Okay, no more sadness!" I smiled. "Plus, I am dying for you to tell me what you got on Professor Greenfield's exam."

"A-," she brushed off pretend dirt on her left shoulder.

"You bitch," I laughed. "I only got a B+!"

Just then, Aaron entered the bar and made a beeline for us.

"Amalia!" he grabbed me off the stool and pulled me in for a big hug. "Happy birthday, sis!"

"It's so good to see you!" I beamed. "I want to hear about everything. How's school? Oh! Let me introduce you to Hayden."

I knew it must have upset Hayden a bit that I didn't introduce him as my boyfriend, but he took it in his stride and happily shook my brother's hand. The two of them started talking about basketball, and I knew they would get along just fine.

Following Aaron's arrival, Cassandra strutted in with her cell phone pressed to her ear. Of course. I caught her eye and waved. She hung up just as she approached me and pulled me in for a tight hug.

"Happy birthday, girl," she said in my ear. "You look great."

"Thanks!" I tipped my crown at her. "No Brandon tonight?"

She shook her head. "We ended things."

"I'm sorry to hear that. Are you alright?" I asked. Even though she and I hadn't spoken much recently, Cassie was still important to me.

"Oh yeah, I'm fine!" she said, deflecting. "Oh and by the way," she pulled me in closer and whispered into my ear. "Michael's outside."

I felt a sudden shortness of breath, followed by a general

166

queasiness. Had that Cosmopolitan made me sick? No, I don't think I drank nearly enough of it to have affected me.

Cassandra squeezed my shoulder and excused herself to use the ladies' room, but I hardly heard a word she said. For a moment, I was sitting alone. Olivia had stepped outside to have a smoke, Hayden was deep in conversation about the Knicks with Aaron, and Cassandra was in the restroom. And in walked Michael. Alone. He caught eyes with me and smiled. It felt like the room was in slow motion as he walked over to me. Even with Hayden right by my side, I couldn't deny the effect Michael had over me any longer. As much as I hated to admit it, I couldn't deny the truth from myself anymore. I was right back where I was last year.

I was still in love with Michael.

Midnight came and I was uncomfortably seated at a small, round table in the back corner of the bar. The table was wood and splintery, poking tiny holes in my stockings every time I moved. Yet another LMFAO song was playing and through my tipsy haze I yelled, "Come on! Turn that crap off!"

Hayden and Michael both laughed at my drunkenness, but I was nowhere near as bad as Olivia. I saw her taking shots of vodka with some tall, dark and handsome stranger she had met about an hour ago. The two of them were getting cozy by the bar, as the mystery dude had her sandwiched between a bar stool and his hips. She was giggling and appeared flirtatious, but as I watched her take her fourth vodka shot, I worried about her judgment.

Cassandra had been AWOL for most of the night. The last time anyone saw her was at around 10:30 pm when she stepped outside to make a phone call. Aaron told me she came back into the bar 45 minutes later, bleary-eyed and puffy-lipped. Apparently whoever she was on the phone with had made her very upset.

Aaron had also spent most of the night solo after catching the eye of a cute girl. She looked around the same age as him, 21, and definitely appeared to be dressed that way. She had on a super- short, hot-pink skirt with high-heeled strappy sandals. A bold choice of outfit for a breezy October night. I hadn't heard about him dating anyone since he showed up to my apartment in shambles last year, so I figured I'd leave him to it and let him have some fun.

As unexpected as it was, Hayden, Michael, and I were seated at the table by ourselves. The more Michael and Hayden got along, the guiltier I felt about not telling Hayden the whole story about our past. I was caught in the middle. Literally. The table was small and the bar was over-crowded. Both of their knees were pressed up against mine. Hayden's I knew was deliberate, he also held my hand. I felt a mix of happiness and anxiety as Hayden held my hand, but I couldn't help but wonder about Michael's positioning. I looked around as I was sipping my third Jack and ginger. Between Cassandra's absence, Olivia's drunkenness, and Hayden and Michael's bonding, I was resolved to call it a night.

Just as I was about to tell the guys I wasn't going to be able to have another drink, I heard a girl yelling over by the bar. The three of us snapped around in our chairs to witness Olivia, firmly pressed up against the bar by the unknown guy. He had one hand on her arm and the other on her waist. He was trying to pull her in for a kiss as she used her free arm to push him off. He ignored her pleas and continued with his unwanted advances.

The bartender was nowhere to be seen, and no one else in the bar seemed to care or notice Olivia's distress. Michael and Hayden both rose the moment the word "stop" escaped Olivia's lips. Her hazel eyes were wide and her red lipstick was smudged. Michael darted toward her and angrily tapped her pursuant on the shoulder. The guy turned around and finally let go of Olivia's wrist. As soon as he faced Michael, the guy's lips twisted into a smirk. Olivia immediately rubbed her wrist and darted over toward me and Hayden. Michael stood about three inches taller than the blonde, fraternity-looking guy, who just moments ago was trying to pressure our friend to leave the bar with him. I felt nervous as

I watched Michael take a step closer to him. I couldn't hear their conversation. The chatter in the bar was loud; the music was even louder. I grabbed Hayden's hand for support. He just looked at me and then took a step forward to help Michael out. I pulled him back. I didn't want to risk them both getting into a fight. I wasn't sure what Michael was going to do, but I suddenly realized I worried for his safety.

Just then, the blonde guy shoved Michael, forcing him to fall into a neighboring booth. Michael regained his footing and shoved the guy back, knocking him into the bar stool he just had Olivia pressed up on. For a moment the two of them just stared at each other, silently daring the other to throw the first punch. The moment was up. The blonde took a step forward and took a swing. Michael ducked and the guy ended up hitting nothing but the air. He swung at Michael again, his fist colliding with Michael's face this time. Michael stepped back and tested his jaw. He had a small amount of blood in the corner of his mouth that was now on his hand. Swinging back, Michael hit the frat guy. Hard. He fell backwards onto the floor. As he fell, he dragged the stool down with him. He was down.

"Let's get out of here!" I said, feeling a mixture of anxiety and fear. Michael hopped backwards and rejoined us at the table, just in time for us to duck out of the bar. From what I could tell, the blonde guy was still on the ground when we left.

We jogged until we were around the corner and completely out of sight from the bar. Olivia bent down and hugged herself. She slowly sat on the pavement and burst into tears. I bent down beside her and gently stroked her hair.

"It's okay," I said in a comforting tone. "It's over now."

I saw a male figure round the corner and thought it was the guy coming back for seconds. I felt my blood run cold, but once the guy came into view, I realized the blonde hair belonged to my brother.

"Oh my God," he puffed. "All I saw was Michael punch some

169

guy. Are you girls alright?"

I nodded, still bent over, but motioned toward Olivia. She was clearly not alright.

I looked up at Michael, his lip was puffy and there was a bluish bruise forming on the left side of his jaw. "Thank you," I uttered.

"Of course," he said. "What a piece of shit that guy was. I swear if I ever see him again-"

"Just be glad it's done with," Hayden cut in. "You did the right thing, man."

"Thanks," Michael uttered.

Olivia was still crying on the ground, moaning drunkenly about Alex and how she wanted to go home. I stroked her hair again and looked back up at the guys.

"Michael," I said. "Do you think you can make sure she gets home safely?"

"Of course."

"I'll go with you too," Aaron offered.

Hayden, Aaron, and I helped Olivia to her feet as Michael stood by the corner, desperately trying to hail a cab.

"I ruined your birthday," she mumbled. "I'm so sorry."

"No," I answered quickly. "You didn't ruin anything. Don't say that. I am just glad you're okay."

A cab rolled up and without unlocking its doors asked Michael where he was headed. I could just barely make out the cab driver's face as he shook his head, indicating that he, like most cab drivers, was not up for making the trip to Brooklyn.

"Look, I don't care if you don't want to drive to Brooklyn!" Michael shouted. I recoiled a bit. I had never heard him raise his voice before. "This is an emergency. She needs to get home."

The cab driver thought about it for a moment and then unlocked his doors. Michael opened the back door and he and Aaron carefully placed Olivia into the back seat. Aaron sat next to her and Michael slid next to him.

"Thank you," I called out. Michael just nodded.

"I'll text you when we get to her apartment," Aaron declared. A few seconds later, the cab driver pulled away.

I breathed a sigh of relief and let my head fall into my hands. "What in the world just happened?" I uttered silently.

Hayden pulled me in for a hug and just held me. I felt tears welling up in my eyes, scared for my friend. Freaked-out from what I had just witnessed, but I tried to hold it together.

"Do you want me to take you home?" Hayden asked, still holding me tightly.

"I don't want to go there," I said, still shaken up from what happened at the bar. "I want to go to *your* apartment."

"Whatever you want, birthday girl." Hayden unlocked his arms and stepped to the corner to hail a cab.

"Yeah," I snickered. "Some fucking birthday."

"I'm sorry it ended like this," he said. "Let me take you to brunch tomorrow. Just you and me."

"That would be nice," I forced a smile.

We stood impatiently in the chilly fall air for about ten minutes until a cab finally pulled over. Hayden gave him his address, and being that it was within the city limits, the cab driver didn't give him a hard time. He held the door open for me and I slid across the tattered back seat. He reached for my hand and I could feel his eyes on me as I stared out the window. I kept my eyes straight, staring out the window the entire time, until we reached his apartment.

Chapter 24

Olivia

"Are you going to that big parade they have in the Village every year?" my dad asked.

I was lying in a robe on my couch, slowly sipping a glass of water. My dad had called me to see how I was doing. He was always good like that; always looking out for me. Even though my mother and I have a strained relationship, I knew I could always count on my father. I told him about Alex. How we broke up. How I felt as if it was my fault. And how I hadn't left the apartment, with the exception of going to class, since Amalia's birthday. More than two weeks had passed since then, and today was Halloween. It was also the last day to apply for Dr. Greenfield's work-study program. I had the paperwork all filled out and, come hell or high water, I was handing in my application today after class.

"No, I think I am going to skip it this year," I replied.

"You really should get out and have some fun," he said. "I don't like the idea of you cooped up in that apartment all by yourself." I could hear the sadness in his voice.

I didn't want to tell my dad that the last time I went out and tried to have fun, a certain frat-looking guy had gotten a little too hands-on with me. I was in a crappy mood because the truth was, I usually loved watching the Halloween parade in the Village.

But this year I just couldn't find the energy to go out. I was still embarrassed from what happened at Amalia's birthday party. The guys had gotten me home safe that night, and I woke up to find Aaron asleep on my couch. I thanked him profusely for watching out for me and he told me I did him a favor by not making him spend money on a hotel room that night.

"I'm alright," I uttered. "I have to go to class today anyway and I'll probably be too exhausted from doing schoolwork to go out tonight."

"Just try to do something fun this weekend, okay?"

I smiled. My dad knew the right thing to say. He didn't push me for details on my and Alex's break-up, but I still knew he was there for me anytime I needed him. My mom and I only talked every couple of months. We didn't have a very close relationship. In some ways, I think she was envious of my and my father's closeness.

"I'll try," I said. "What about you? When are you going to find yourself a nice woman to date?"

My dad started stammering into the phone, like he always did when I teased him about dating. He and my mom had been divorced for a very long time, but he still didn't like to talk to me about the women he went out with. I guess I didn't really need to hear all of it. I just wanted my dad to find someone to make him happy.

"I'm not seeing anyone right now," he said quickly.

"I'm just teasing you, Dad."

"I know you are. I just don't want you to worry about me. I'm fine on my own. Oh and sweetheart, I know it's not my place," he began. "But if you really feel like this Alex guy is the one for you, then you should try to make it work."

The only communication Alex and I had had in the past month was when I dropped my pen walking to my seat in class and he picked it up for me. He no longer sat in our row. It was unbearable to see him nearly every day and not be able to talk to him. I was starting to think my dad was right. I had done enough sulking.

174

Alex had to know that Nate was nothing to me. He had to know I knew I was wrong for hiding it from him, and that I missed him every single day.

"Thanks, Dad," I forced a smile. "I may just do that."

I got to Dr. Greenfield's class five minutes before it began. Surprisingly, there were a lot of empty seats. I walked toward the middle rows, where my friends usually took over. As I tiptoed closer, I noticed that Alex once again wasn't sitting with them. Michael was seated in between Angela and Amalia, who was busy texting someone. Since our break-up, Alex had opted to sit in the back. Easier to sneak in and out, I suppose. I scanned the room looking for him; he hadn't arrived yet. Walking back out of the classroom, I stood in the hallway, deciding I would cut him off at the entrance.

A minute later I heard the ding of the elevator and out stepped Alex. He was dressed nicely, wearing his usual dark-wash jeans and a designer button-down, but his eyes were worn out, and his hair was a mess. He noticed me and put his head down, crossing over to the classroom entrance.

"Hey," I uttered.

He stopped in his tracks. Still looking down, he didn't answer me. Finally he cleared his throat and said hi.

"Listen," I said, trying to sound as sweet as possible. "I was hoping you and I could talk."

"Talk about what?" he asked sharply. Still looking down. In the background we could hear Dr. Greenfield's voice booming over the microphone. My anxiety kicked up a notch as I realized I was most likely going to be late for class.

"I wanted to talk to you about us," I uttered.

"What about us?" he asked, softer now. He looked up at me and pursed his lips.

"I'm sorry," I said. "Can we please talk about what happened? Face to face?"

Alex just stood there for a moment. Someone from one of the

back rows stood up to close the classroom doors. He noticed Alex and I standing there and asked if we were in or out.

"We're coming," Alex snapped. The guy stepped back and put up both of his hands as he returned to his seat.

"So what do you say?" I asked again. "How's tomorrow?"

"Sure," he finally answered. "Come by my apartment around 8."

"Perfect," I said. I felt like jumping for joy, but I restrained myself. Alex made an "after you" motion with his hand and I walked into the classroom.

I looked back, expecting him to follow me to the middle row where our friends were seated, but he stayed in the back. Baby steps, I thought as I took an empty seat next to Angela.

"You're late," she whispered.

"It's okay," I said. "It was worth it."

The next night I splurged for a cab and rode it all the way from Park Slope to Roosevelt Island. I had barely gone out the past few weeks, so I had the extra cash. I was shocked that the cab driver had agreed to go that far, but I told him I'd tip him very well if he didn't make me take the subway. I slipped him forty bucks when we pulled up to Alex's apartment building.

I hadn't even realized I was holding my breath until I let out a long, breathy sigh. I was so nervous to see him. I smoothed over my dress and my hair as I stepped out of the cab. Taking the deepest of breaths I immediately craved a cigarette. Shaking it off, I fought past the craving. I wanted to arrive smelling like my new Marc Jacobs perfume, not like an ashtray. When I reached Alex's apartment, I put my hand into my purse to retrieve the key he gave me halfway into our relationship, but then stopped myself. I hadn't given the key back because I was holding out hope that we'd get back together. Still, we had broken up. I had no right to just walk into his home anymore. So I rolled my hand into a fist and for the first time in over six months knocked on Alex's door.

He waited a few seconds before letting me in.

"It was open," he said.

"I didn't want to just impose," I uttered.

"No imposition," he replied, flatly. He looked very serious, and I couldn't tell if he actually wanted me in his apartment or not. He walked over to the counter, where two wine glasses were waiting. "Would you like a glass?"

"Definitely," I said, placing my purse up on the counter. I silently willed my heartbeat to slow down.

Alex poured us both a glass of Pinot Noir and gave me a weak smile. It was incredibly awkward. I numbly followed him to the couch, where he immediately put down his wine glass and lit up a cigarette. So much for not smelling like an ashtray.

"Olivia," he said. "What did you want to talk to me about?"

I looked down for a moment and began to wonder if I had made the wrong choice coming here. Alex was acting so cold. So distant.

"I actually came here to apologize," I said without looking at him.

Alex said nothing. He pulled another drag of his cigarette and swirled his Pinot around in his chalice-sized glass. I figured by the way he was acting I had nothing to lose.

"Alex," I said, directly facing him this time. "I'm in love with you and I miss you."

He stopped swirling and finally caught my eye. The moment he looked at me I started to cry.

"I should have told you about running into Nate," I said through sobs. "But all of that's in my past. I'm not that person anymore."

"What person?" he asked quietly.

"The person who lets themselves get dragged around by some guy just because the sex is good."

Alex's eyes went wide.

"I'm sorry," I said, lightly hitting myself on the head. "I know that sounds crude, but that's who I used to be."

Alex put out his cigarette and I took the opportunity to reach for his hands.

"I thought I loved Nate. I thought all of the fighting, the

177

sneaking around, and the passion was because we were in love. I thought that's what love was. But I could not have been more wrong."

For a moment, I thought I saw Alex's eyes start to well up. "Go on," he said.

"I think us girls get confused by it. But that's not what love is. Love is knowing someone is going to be there for you on your worst days. It's when you know that someone truly is busy if they don't contact you all day because they would never play games with you. Most importantly, love is what I have with you. So, Alex, please tell me that you still love me."

Without missing a beat he answered, "I never stopped. I just thought I couldn't compete with what you two had in your past."

"I don't care about him," I said. I realized that sounded harsh, but it was true. "I just want us to get back together."

Before I could say another word, Alex kissed me. I started to cry harder, and he picked up his hand and wiped away my tears.

"I have always loved you, Olivia."

I lightly pressed my forehead against his, still gripping tightly onto his hands.

"Let's go away somewhere," he said.

"What?" I laughed. "Where?"

"Anywhere," he kissed me. "Let's take a cab to La Guardia and go somewhere tonight. Just you and me. It's Thursday night and we don't have classes on Fridays. We'll come back Sunday evening. You won't miss anything."

"I don't want to miss anything ever again," I replied, but I wasn't talking about school.

"Miami," he whispered in my ear. "It's only a three-hour flight."

"I'll go anywhere with you," I smiled. I was nodding so hard my entire body was shaking.

Neither of us said another word. I grabbed my purse off the kitchen table and laughed as Alex haphazardly threw clothes into a duffle bag. When he was finished, he grabbed my hand and we raced downstairs, hailing the first cab we saw.

Chapter 25

Amalia

I woke up to the smell of freshly brewed coffee, which was odd because I didn't own a coffee-maker. By the beginning of November, I was finally unpacked, furnished (barely), and no longer living like a crazy bag lady. And last night, for the first time since we started dating, I let Hayden spend the night at my place. After seeing Michael at my birthday party, I was trying my best to put any thoughts about him out of my mind. It was much easier to do when Hayden was around.

I sat up in bed and stretched out. My shades had already been opened, as was the door to my bedroom. Slipping on some socks, I made my way into my tiny hallway, where Hayden stood holding two cups of coffee and a copy of the *New York Times*.

"I thought I smelled coffee," I said through a groggy voice, as he handed me a cup. "I see you got the paper."

Hayden and I walked over to my new couch, which I ended up getting on sale at Target. I pulled my five-dollar, geometric-print pillow up to my chest and yawned. He flipped through the pages until he reached the wedding section.

"My cousin submitted her wedding announcement a long time ago and I wanted to check if she got in," his eyes scanned the paper. Getting your wedding announced in the *New York Times* was very

181

important to New Yorkers. The rumor was, you'd have an easier time getting struck by lightning than having your announcement printed in their Sunday edition. "Ah! Here it is!" He hit the paper with his hand and laughed.

"You didn't go to the wedding?" I asked.

"I couldn't get the time off of work unfortunately," he shrugged.

I peered over his shoulder and read the blurb. The couple's picture was identical to every other. The two of them were seated, their shoulders were perfectly aligned, and their heads were somehow, despite any height differences, at the same level.

"Lucky bitch," I joked as I sipped my coffee.

"Seriously," he laughed, as he folded the paper and tossed it back on the table.

I scanned the paragraph under their picture. "Can you imagine having such a huge wedding?" I asked. "That announcement said she had about 350 guests. I don't even know that many people."

"No way," he agreed. "When I get married, I want it to be quiet. Just close friends and family. Maybe somewhere with a beach.

"That sounds lovely," I nodded. "I've never been one for big spectacles."

"Speaking of relationships, how are Olivia and Alex doing?"

"They're great," I said with a chuckle. "They're back from Miami now. Can you believe they just grabbed the first flight out completely spontaneously?"

"What did she do for clothes?"

"He bought her clothes when they landed!" I laughed. "The whole thing is like out of a movie. It must be nice to be rich."

"Is she rich?" he asked.

"No," I shook my head. "Alex is rich. Well, his family is anyway."

"Right." Hayden put his coffee down and turned to me. "So not to change the subject, but I was wondering what your plans were for Thanksgiving?"

"Well, nothing big," I answered. "I'm just going to go to my parents' house in Staten Island. I'm sure Aaron will be there too.

Like I said, I'm not one for big spectacles."

Hayden laughed and put his arm around me. "I was going to see if you wanted to come down to Florida for the weekend, and spend the holiday with me and my family. I know Gainesville isn't exactly Miami, but it will be warm there. And we can still treat it like a mini-vacation."

Suddenly, the *room* felt very warm, despite the barely working heat. I put down my coffee cup, which now felt burning hot, and scooted over a bit on the couch.

"It wouldn't be fair to my family," I muttered, twisting a curl through my fingers. "I see them so infrequently."

Hayden had a slightly pained look on his face. I could tell he was hoping for a more positive response.

"It's not a problem," he smiled through sad eyes.

"Are you sure?" I asked. I was worried he would take it as a blow-off.

"Of course," he kissed my hand. "So what do you want to do today?"

I was glad for the change of subject. "How about we finish our coffees and then go somewhere for brunch?"

"Sounds great."

I offered him a kiss and leaned back into him. I didn't know what I was doing. The truth was, my parents probably wouldn't mind if I didn't go home for Thanksgiving, but Hayden and I weren't even officially a couple. Completely on my part, not his. Going all the way to Florida for a big national holiday seemed like a bit much. Hayden stroked my hair as we sat in silence for a few moments. I felt my heartbeat return to normal, and reached for my coffee, which was now the perfect temperature. As soon as I felt at ease, an unwanted thought crept into my mind. I wish I could block these questions out, but they always seem to seep through at the most unexpected moments. As I leaned against my perfect guy I couldn't stop myself from wondering, what were Michael's plans for Thanksgiving?

As the final leaves fell, the holiday approached and I found myself once again riding the ferry home to Staten Island. The ride was always the same length, 25 minutes long, but each time I took it I swore it had gotten longer. Even with the newest Sara Shepard book in hand, I found it hard to relax. Hayden had left to go back to Gainesville two days before, boarding an early-morning flight. I spent a lot of time thinking about him when he left. We still weren't in a relationship, and he hadn't even brought it up again since my birthday over a month ago. I knew the ball was entirely in my court, and as I let my mind drift it kept coming back around to Michael. He was dating Angela, but not really. I was dating Hayden, but I couldn't commit. I really cared about Hayden, so why did I keep thinking about Michael?

I leaned back against the hard seat on the boat and decided to pop on my earphones instead of reading.

Twenty-five endless minutes and four Mumford & Sons songs later, the ferry docked and I saw my brother waving at me inside the terminal.

"Howdy," I smiled. "Long time no see."

"I know," he said, helping me with my overnight bag. "But frankly, I'm kind of sick of you."

He was obviously joking, but I still offered him my best eye-roll. "Apparently you're not the only one," I grimaced.

"What do you mean?"

I gave him a sideways look. "Cassandra."

I hadn't seen Cassandra since her brief pop-in at my birthday get-together. I had invited her to take the ferry back into Staten Island with me, assuming she would be seeing her family for Thanksgiving.

She never called me back.

He shook his head and we headed toward his car. "Who the hell knows what's going on with that girl? Even her Twitter has been completely untouched for the past two weeks."

"Okay, that's a sign of trouble. When I get back to the city I have to try and sit her down and find out why she's acting like this," I said.

"Do you think it's something serious?"

"Yeah, she's *seriously* obsessed with her job and making money. To the point where she's completely alienated her best friend."

Aaron slid into the driver's seat. "It's her loss," he offered.

"Anyway, thanks for picking me up," I said, changing the subject. "It was either that or brace myself for the Staten Island Rail Road."

"No sister of mine is going to risk a mugging on Thanksgiving!" he said. "Besides, this car *is* technically yours."

I mindlessly flipped through the radio stations on the way home and Aaron chatted my ear off about college, wanting to go back to his internship in Manhattan after the school year was over, and the girl he met at my birthday.

"I got her number, but I did sort of run out on her after the fight broke out," he explained.

Fifteen minutes later we pulled up to my parents' house. The second I closed the car door, I was greeted by my father in a frenzy.

"Amalia," my dad came rushing out of the house. "Is everything okay between you and Hayden?"

I looked at my brother, who just shrugged.

"Yes," I stammered. "Why?" I closed the car door and crossed my arms.

My dad put his arm around me and whispered in my ear. "Well, you know your mother told me that he's not coming for Thanksgiving." He started walking me toward the front door.

"That's right," I said in full volume, not sure why he was whispering. "He's in Florida with his own annoying family."

I walked into the house and was immediately hit with the scent of turkey, cornbread, and fresh cranberries. My mouth filled with water. I hadn't had a home-cooked meal since Nick and I were dating. The idea of signing up for couple of cooking classes came to mind as a Christmas present for Hayden. Even though we weren't "officially" in a relationship, there was no reason we

185

couldn't still do something fun for the two of us.

"You see, Amalia," my dad continued, his arm still around my shoulders. "It would just be a shame if the two of you broke up. You know, without knowing if you were both truly compatible. It could have been a mistake to let him go."

"What are you talking about?" I wasn't home for ten seconds and I was already being ambushed by one overbearing parent. Just listening to this line of random questioning from my father reminded me why I opted to pay so much money for my apartment in the West Village last year.

"Amalia? Is that you?" my mom shouted from the kitchen.

"Yeah, it's me!" I took a step forward to sneak some food, but my dad stopped me.

"I'm talking about how to know if someone is really right for you, Amalia," my dad led me to the couch, ignoring my mother. Aaron plopped down on the chair across from us, folded his hands in his lap and smiled. He was clearly enjoying this.

"We aren't in a relationship, Dad, we are still just in the dating phase."

"Good!" my dad jumped up, nearly knocking over a turkey-shaped display dish in the process, and ran over to a small desk in the corner of the living room. "Then there's still time."

"What are you talking about? Still time for-" but I stopped myself. I knew exactly what he was talking about. I snapped my head over to Aaron, who was barely holding it together at this point. I turned back to my father, who was rifling through papers. "Dad, no."

It was too late, he had already found it and was now holding it in his hand like a prize. Freshly printed off the computer this morning was the Test. The stupid, invasive, borderline harassing test that my father had come up with to give my high-school boyfriends to make sure they were good enough for me. I pressed my lips into a straight line and wondered what time the next ferry back to Manhattan was.

"You see, Amalia," he reached into his coat pocket for his glasses. "It's very important that you get certain questions out of the way when you first meet someone. It's only a precaution, to see if you're compatible. Just simple questions like 'Where did you go to college?' and 'What's your credit score?' You know, nothing too invasive."

"Is that so?" I snatched the paper, excuse me *papers*, out of my father's hand, flipped to page number 5 and read aloud from it. "Question number 46- have you in the past, or would you ever in the future donate a kidney?" I placed the stack of papers in my lap and looked up at my father. "How exactly is knowing the answer to that going to help me in my relationship?"

"It shows that he would donate a kidney for you if you needed one!" my father defended. "And if he already gave one up, you know to kick him to the curb because-"

"Because he doesn't have any viable organs to give me?" I cut him off.

My father just glared at me. "I'll admit, that one's a little extreme," he offered.

I flipped back to page 3. "Question number 27- if you were forced to kill one member of your family, or be killed yourself, who would you choose and why?"

My dad just stared at me. Completely still, unflappable. The sound of my mother setting the table in the next room was the only thing we heard for a few seconds.

"Just take it home with you," he said. "Show it Hayden."

"I'm going to get a drink," I stood up and walked into the kitchen.

"I'm coming with you," Aaron followed, tears from laughing running down his face. "Happy Thanksgiving, sis!"

I shook my head and sat down at the kitchen table. My mother was wearing pearl earrings, a geometric-patterned apron, a knee-length dress with sheer stockings, and her blonde hair pulled back into a tight ponytail. She handed me a can of diet soda and smiled.

Not exactly the kind of drink I had in mind.

"Why are you dressed like an extra on Mad Men?" I asked her.

"It's a holiday, Amalia," she said while looking my own outfit up and down. I was wearing jeans and a blouse. I guess I could have put on a dress, but it was already pretty cold in November and being on the ferry only made it more unbearable. "Most people get dressed up."

Aaron, who was also wearing jeans, sat next to me and my mother sat down on the other side of him. My dad, still standing, began to carve the turkey.

"Now doesn't that smell delicious?" my dad smiled. "And don't you kids worry, we made extra stuffing this year."

Aaron, still laughing, just shook his head.

"Now," my mother said, folding her hands in her lap. "Who wants to say what they're thankful for?"

I grimaced and pointed toward Aaron.

"Amalia," my mother smiled. "Why don't you begin?"

My brother leaned over to me and whispered, "I bet you're wishing you had gone to Florida with Hayden right about now."

I smiled and tried to think of something polite to say to my parents, all the while thinking that I was really thankful for the fact that I would only have to spend one night with them.

Chapter 26

Olivia

"I already told you why I don't want to do anything for New Year's Eve," I said, flipping through my Social Psychology notes. "It's lame, it's cold, and it's extremely overpriced."

Alex just stared at me like I had grown a fifth head.

"Look, I know you like to party and soak in all that New York City has to offer every chance you get, but please don't make me go out this year on New Year's Eve. If you want to go out with Michael and Angela to whatever club they're hitting up, I don't mind. Just please let me stay home."

The winter had flown by and it was already the middle of December, downright late to most New Yorkers to start making plans for New Year's Eve. No one understood why I hated this holiday. It was just so over-hyped. And especially in a city that is already so pumped up on self- ingratiating pomp and circumstance, I honestly would rather spend the night with a glass of wine in a bubble bath. That was, if I had a bathtub. A glass of wine in my stand-up shower would just be plain gross.

"Even Amalia wants to go out," Alex said, practically whining. He was pacing back in forth in my apartment. "And she hates all of this shit. Come on, just give me a little something."

I was holding my ground. Every year my friends dragged me

out to some bar or club on New Year's and I spent the entire night miserable, and the entire next day throwing up.

"We're not even up to Christmas yet and you're already planning New Year's Eve?"

"What can I say?" he said. "I like to get a jump-start on things. Plus we're both just staying here for Christmas. It's going to be completely lame."

I lowered my notes and shot him a look.

"I mean romantic," he stammered.

I shook my head and let out a snort. "Didn't you get enough excitement spending Thanksgiving with my dad in Rhode Island?"

"No." he said. "Don't get me wrong. The food was delicious and I love your father and fall foliage, but this is New Year's Eve, baby!"

"I'll tell you what," I said, pressing my hands into my temples. "We can go out to dinner, but that's it. Please?"

Alex stopped pacing and sat down next to me. He let out a soft sigh and began to rub my shoulders. A good distraction technique.

"You drive a hard deal, Miss Davis. But I believe we can come to a compromise," he said, brushing my brown hair off of my back to get better access to my shoulders.

"What deal would that be?"

"We can go out to dinner, anywhere you'd like. Even if it happens to be McDonalds. But after dinner, instead of coming straight home, we get a suite at the Mandarin Oriental hotel overlooking the park."

Now I couldn't possibly say no to that. The Mandarin Oriental Hotel was located in Columbus Circle. It was one of the nicest hotels in the entire city, and it claimed the best views of Central Park to boot. But I didn't want Alex to know he had won me over so quickly. I sat in silence for a moment, pretending to think it over.

"Okay," I said, throwing my hands up. "You've twisted my arm!"

Alex stood up and took an over-the-top bow. I laughed and pulled on his shirt until he was low enough to kiss me.

"Thank you," he said. "I promise you, you won't regret it."

"Well, if you're finished, can I get back to studying now?" I held up my notebook. "You know, our final is in two days."

"Man, this semester just flew by," he reached for his textbook and sat back down. "I think I'll join you."

"Dr. Greenfield said that since I applied to his research program late, my acceptance is contingent upon my grade on the final exam," I made a pouty face.

"What does your grade have to be?"

"At least an A-," I sighed.

"And the program doesn't begin until next semester, correct?"

"That's what he said," I shrugged. "So plenty of time to worry about it over winter break."

He rubbed my back a bit. "You're going to be great."

I wasn't sure if he was trying to distract me again, but either way I was fully incapable of looking at my books any longer.

"I'm so glad we're back together," I said, pulling him in for another kiss. Everything had been going perfectly since Alex and I got back together last month. Now if I could just get through this final exam, I'd be floating on air.

He put my face in both of his hands and looked deep into my eyes. I felt the warm rush of love wash over me as he kissed me again. Slowly this time.

"We'll never be apart again," he whispered.

"I love you," I said, dropping my book to the floor.

"I thought you had to study?" he murmured in my ear. Then moved onto kissing it.

"Forget that," I jumped into his lap. With one swift movement he lifted me up and carried me into the bedroom.

"Oh yeah," he said, as he lightly placed me on my bed. "I am so glad we are back together."

Chapter 28

Amalia

I let out a deep sigh as I handed my test booklet to the T.A. There was a mixture of reactions among the cohort. Some students were smiling, obviously confident that they had aced Dr. Greenfield's final exam. Others were just staring at the floor in front of them, every so often mumbling incoherently.

I noticed Olivia wink at Alex, so I assumed she did well. The two of them had been in their own little world since they had gotten back together. I was happy for them; they deserved it.

"I hate this place," I mumbled under my breath. "Stupid final."

As I walked out of the classroom, Michael slowly jogged up to me and tapped me on the shoulder.

"How'd you do?" he asked, walking out with me.

I spun around and knocked my bag into him.

"I'm sorry!" I said, scrambling to make sure he was okay, while really hoping he hadn't just heard me talking to myself. Although Michael and I had agreed to be friends, we weren't really doing a bang-up job of it. Apart from class, we never saw each other.

"It's okay. I'm fine!" he laughed, putting his arms on my shoulders to straighten me out. "So what did you think of the exam?"

"I think I got a solid B."

"Could be worse," he shrugged. We continued to walk through

the hallway. I spotted two girls from my class in the corner crying. "And just think, Social Psych is over and you never have to see Dr. Greenfield's face again."

I laughed. "That would be true except I was accepted into his research-study program. So starting in February, I'll be seeing him all of the time."

Michael stopped me just as we exited onto the street. The cold wind immediately slapped us in the face.

"I didn't know you were officially accepted," he smiled widely. "That's great news. Congratulations."

A couple of students from class turned and looked at us. For the first time ever, Michael was being loud.

"Thanks!" I said. I knew it was good news, but somehow hearing it from Michael made it seem more important.

"Who else got accepted?" he buttoned up his pea coat.

"Well, like he said. There's only three spots available. There's me, probably Olivia, and someone named August."

"What do you mean by probably?" he asked, pulling a pair of gloves out of his pocket.

I pulled my scarf around me a little tighter. New York in December was unbearably cold. It seemed like every year it got colder earlier and stayed cold for longer. "Olivia was really down while she and Alex were broken up," I explained. "She didn't hand in her work-study papers until really late in the game. Now the professor is making her jump through hoops."

Michael just nodded.

"So I'm done for the day if you want to go grab lunch or something," he said. "My treat, to celebrate."

I paused for a moment, unsure of what to do. I was meant to meet up with Hayden for lunch at the Shake Shack in Madison Square Park. I opened my mouth to speak and as if on cue, my phone buzzed with a message from him asking if I was on my way.

Michael must have noticed my apprehension, because he took a step back. "Hey, if you already have plans-"

"No," I cut him off. "I'm free. Let's just go somewhere around here, though. I'm freezing and want to get inside!" I quickly texted Hayden back and told him I had to stay late at school. I felt horrible; it was the only time I had ever lied to him. Apart from the giant lie of omission when it came to not telling him the whole story about Michael and me. But I reminded myself, more likely *justified* to myself, that we weren't in a relationship. Besides, it was way too cold to have lunch outside by Shake Shack.

Michael and I found some spot that looked good for lunch and were seated in a booth by a window. I felt a bead of sweat roll down my back, anxiety that I might get caught. I shook myself out of it. Get caught doing what? Having lunch with my friend?

As I scanned the menu, the waiter materialized and asked us what we'd like to drink.

My nerves got the better of me and I ordered a glass of wine. Michael did the same.

"So," he said. "Are you spending Christmas with Cassandra again this year?"

That was a really good question. Today was December 21st, a mere three days until Christmas Eve. By now I would usually know what time I was expected to arrive at her house. I would have already bought her gift at a Black Friday sale, and had it wrapped waiting for her. But this year she had yet to reach out to me, and I felt a little weird about calling her and inviting myself.

"Honestly, I don't know," I admitted. "Things have been a little tense with us these past few months, and I have no idea why."

"Have you tried talking to her about it?"

"I have," I said. "We got into a quasi-argument in a restaurant, but she told me it was neither the time nor the place and essentially walked out on me. She made a brief appearance at my birthday party and then spent the entire night on the phone. I haven't seen her since."

"I hope you two can work it out," he grimaced. His brown eyes widened as his lips twisted and offered me a sympathetic half-smile.

"Me too," I said softly. "But if we don't, it looks like I am spending Christmas here by myself."

"Your parents don't celebrate, right?" he asked.

I shook my head.

"What about Hayden?"

"He actually has to travel for work," I said. "I feel terrible for him. He's leaving tomorrow and will be gone until New Year's Day."

"I'm sorry," Michael cocked his head to the side.

"Don't be!" I waved him off. "I have Home Alone and Love Actually on Blu-ray. I'll be totally fine."

"Well, sounds like you've got it all figured out then," he laughed.

"Now if I can just figure out what to order," I mumbled.

"You were right about Angela," Michael said abruptly as he put down his menu.

"Right about what?" I asked, slightly caught off guard.

"What you told me, at the coffee house, you were right. She just wanted to hook up."

I smiled and leaned my elbows over on to the table. "Does that bother you?"

"Are you a psychologist now?" he laughed. "No, I guess it doesn't. I was just more surprised at how perceptive you are."

"I'll take that as a compliment," I smiled.

The waiter brought us over our drinks and asked us if we were ready to order.

"I think we need another minute," Michael said. The waiter nodded and disappeared. "How are things between you and Hayden?"

My head shot up from my menu. "They're fine," I said slowly. Michael had never asked about Hayden and me before.

Michael smiled and nodded and then returned to his menu. This lunch had gone from friendly to awkward in sixty seconds.

"Can I talk to you?" he said through another sigh.

"We're kind of talking right now," I let out a stream of nervous laughter.

The waiter came back around, but I just shook my head. He gave me a sideways look and huffed away.

"It's just that," he started, "I still think about you."

"What do you mean?" I asked nervously, hoping he would elaborate more. The familiar myriad feelings started flushing in again. I took a sip of my wine, hoping to quell them.

"I just mean, I think about you," he slid his finger along the rim of his wine glass.

Sometimes talking to Michael was like pulling teeth.

"I think about you too," I admitted, although I wasn't sure why.

"I really missed you while you were gone this summer," he said, looking me dead in the eyes.

I felt a wave of heat wash over me. Why was it that every time I had eye contact with this guy, I lost all sense of self-control and reasoning? He was so attractive and suddenly my mind shut off. As if it was too tired to fight with my body any longer.

It was officially giving up.

"I'm not hungry anymore," I whispered.

"Neither am I."

We stared at each other for a moment and I swallowed hard. Michael threw down some cash, grabbed me by the hand, and we darted out of the restaurant. There were a few cabs idly waiting outside. We hopped into the first one that had its light on. As soon as I closed the cab door, Michael grabbed me and pulled me closer. I couldn't control it anymore. I wanted him, and I had since the day I returned from Brazil. I kissed him, vehemently, like if I stopped he would suddenly disappear. Or I would wake up and realize this had all been a dream. He kissed me back with unleashed passion, completely ignoring the cab driver in the front of the car.

When we got to his apartment building, we smoothly walked past the doorman.

"Would you like your mail, Mr. Rathbourne?"

"Not right now, Jonathan," he gave the doorman a small wave. I smiled politely, positive my lipstick was smeared halfway up my cheek.

As soon as we got inside the elevators, Michael lifted me up and pressed me against the wall. For a brief moment, I wondered why I ever stopped doing this. The elevator door opened and he grabbed me by the hand, making a beeline for his apartment. He fumbled with the keys for a moment, but lifted me back up the second the door was unlocked.

We made it to the couch before we were frantically pulling at each other's clothes. I threw my coat and scarf across the room. Michael followed suit. I closed my eyes as he kissed my neck and unbuttoned my blouse.

"You are so sexy," he purred in my ear. I lifted his shirt off in return.

The whole time, he never took his hands off me. Every movement was concupiscent. Passionate. As if we'd never get to see each other again after this encounter.

I looked down and noticed there were no more clothes to peel off. He smiled and lowered himself on top of me. Seconds later we were back to doing what we did best.

Screwing up my life.

Chapter 30

Olivia

"Dinner was delicious," I said to Alex as he helped me take off my coat. "The restaurant was very crowded, though."

"Better than McDonalds?" he said.

"Almost."

We had gone to a late dinner at Serafina, an Italian restaurant on the Upper West Side, and then came directly to the hotel. Alex looked extremely handsome tonight, wearing a classic black suit, crisp white shirt with the top button left undone, and no tie. A look not many men were able to pull off, but he did it with ease.

The suite in the hotel was just as beautiful as I pictured it. It was around 11:30 when we finally arrived. The housekeeping staff had already done turn-down service hours ago, leaving the lights dimmed and the drapes open just enough to see a panoramic view of Columbus Circle. Soft jazz was playing from a small speaker on an end table next to a mosaic lamp. On the coffee table, in the sitting-room area, was a bottle of champagne with a silver ribbon tied on it. I noticed there was a note attached. I crossed over to the table and examined the bottle.

"Compliments of the hotel?" I read the note. "Why would they give us a free bottle of champagne?"

Alex took off his suit jacket and hung it up in the closet next to my coat. "Because they know it's a special night." He glided over to the mini bar and retrieved two champagne flutes.

I kicked off my new Kate Spade shoes; my feet were killing me even though I had barely stood all night. I resolved in the New Year to get used to walking in high heels.

"Are you chiding me again for not wanting to go out and party on New Year's Eve?" I laughed. "I'll make it up to you, okay? I will dress like a slutty leprechaun on Saint Patrick's Day. I'll even bake you some green cupcakes. That sounds kind of gross, actually. Scratch that last part."

"No," he put his arms around me. "I am not giving you a hard time. I knew all along that you hated this holiday and that you wouldn't want to go to some club."

"So you're psychic now?" I asked. "You going to open that bottle, or what?"

"In a minute," he smiled. "I think there are probably some chocolates in the bedroom."

He opened the double doors that led to the bedroom.

"This room is huge," I exclaimed, taking it all in. "I think there are two bathrooms in here. This must have cost you a fortune."

"Worth every penny," he uttered. "Come sit on the bed."

I walked into the bedroom and noticed on the bedside table was a bouquet of what had to be two dozen white roses. Next to that was a box of Godiva chocolates.

"Are those for me?" I asked. Alex just smiled. "They're so beautiful." I bent down to experience their wonderful aroma.

"You see, I knew you wouldn't want to go out tonight," Alex let out a soft chuckle. "In fact, I was kind of banking on it."

"Why is that?" I asked, still admiring the flowers.

"Because I've had this planned since the night we got back together," he said in a slightly shaky voice.

"Had what planned?" I turned around to face Alex and gasped when I saw that he was down on one knee. "Oh my God." I spoke through my hands, which were covering my face. Suddenly it all made sense. The suite at an expensive hotel, the fancy dinner, the champagne, the roses. My eyes began to well with tears as I realized Alex was proposing to me.

"Olivia Davis," he spoke softly and slowly. "I love you more than I have ever loved anyone. Being with you makes me feel more grounded and comfortable in my own skin than I ever thought possible. You are, without a doubt, my one." He reached into his pants pocket and pulled out a small black box. He opened it at the exact moment he said the words, "Will you marry me?"

Without even looking at the ring, I nodded my head. I kept nodding my head until finally I could utter a sound that resembled the word yes. Alex stood up and slid the ring on my left finger. It was gorgeous. From what I could tell, it was a one-carat, brilliant-cut solitaire set in what I was assuming was white gold. It was the prettiest piece of jewelry I had ever seen. And it was all mine.

Alex sat down beside me on the bed and reached for my hand. There were tears in his eyes.

"Are you crying?" I asked through my own sobs. I lightly stroked his dark-blonde hair with my fingertips.

"Can you blame me?" he laughed. "I love you, Olivia Davis."

"Soon to be Olivia Carlson," I couldn't help but admire my ring. I cupped his face with my hands. "You are *my* one."

"I am so fucking happy," he said, inches away from my face. "I think it's time for that champagne now." He got up and darted over to the sitting area and popped open the champagne. It didn't splatter everywhere but the sound was still loud enough to startle me. We were both laughing like children, knowing this was a night we would remember for the rest of our lives.

I floated over to him and as he poured me a glass of shimmering gold liquid I noticed it was snowing outside.

"This city really is magnificent, isn't it?" I whispered. I walked closer to the window and watched the snow blanket Central Park and Columbus Circle. It was the most magical night of my life.

Alex stood next to me, champagne in hand and then checked

his watch.

"Bored of me already?" I joked. 'Oh, it's going to be a long life together if you get bored this easily."

He shook his head and then took a large sip of his champagne. He reached for my glass and put both glasses back on the coffee table.

"What are you doing?"

He put his finger softly up to my lips and then moved in closer. "Three, two, one. Happy New Year." He wrapped his arms around my waist and pulled me in for a kiss. I kissed him back. When we were finished, we just stood there for a moment, wrapped in each other's arms.

"I changed my mind," I said, reaching for the remainder of my champagne. "New Year's Eve is definitely my new favorite holiday."

Chapter 31

Amalia

I spent the next week in hiding. Hayden had gotten home from his trip days ago, but I told him I was sick and it was best if I just stayed home to let it run its course. The more he offered to get me matzoh-ball soup from Junior's, the more I hated myself.

Cassandra never did invite me over for Christmas. I checked her Facebook page a dozen times, going through her pictures with a fine-tooth comb. Growing angrier at each holiday photo that she tagged. Her whole family was in the pictures. The family I used to feel a part of.

I had two missed called from Olivia both complete with voice-mails that I had yet to listen to. I heard my phone buzz and I pulled my blanket tighter over my face. Two seconds later there was a knock at my door.

"Ugh!" I shouted. "Go away."

"Amalia?" said a voice. "It's Olivia. Open up, I have to tell you something!" More urgent knocking.

I groaned as I carried my blanket with me to the front door. "I'm coming." I dragged myself off the couch and made my way to the front door.

"Woah," Olivia said, looking me up and down. "What are you doing?" she walked past me and sat on my Target couch.

"Please come in," I mumbled. "I wasn't doing anything. I was sleeping."

She glanced at the clock on my coffee table. "It's three in the afternoon."

"So what?" I said, covering my head with the blanket. "We're on break from school." I sat down next to her on the couch and whipped the blanket off my face. "Alright," I rubbed my eyes. "I guess there's something I should tell you."

"I have something to tell you too!" she beamed.

"Okay, you go first," I offered.

"No, no. Go ahead."

I pressed my palms to my eyes and shook my head. "I had sex with Michael."

Olivia's face went white, like I just told her I murdered a bunny rabbit. Her hazel eyes were as round as saucers and the complete look of disgust on her face only made me feel worse. I waited for her judgment. For her to tell me how horrible I was, like she did last year when she found out I was sleeping with him.

"I know!' I threw the blanket across the room and unveiled the sweatpants I had been wearing for the past three days. "I am a horrible person, okay? I'm an asshole."

"You cheated on Hayden?" she uttered.

"Technically, no. We aren't really in a relationship," I muttered, as if that technicality made the situation any better.

"What are you going to do?" she asked, putting a supportive hand on my knee. "Are you going to leave Hayden? Do you want to be with Michael?"

I was surprised by her support. I had expected her to rip me a new one. "I honestly have no-" I started to speak, but then something caught my eye. I held up her hand that she had placed on my knee. "Oh my God, what is this? Are you and Alex engaged?"

A smile tugged at the ends of Olivia's mouth until she looked as if she was going to burst. "Yes!"

"And you let me go on and on about my infantile boy drama?" I asked with a smile. "Olivia! I am so happy for you!" I pulled her in for a hug. "When did this happen? And let me get another look at that ring! Wow, it's beautiful."

"Thank you!" she was absolutely glowing. "It happened on New Year's Eve. We went out to dinner and then stayed the night in a hotel. That's where he popped the question."

I was genuinely happy for Olivia. But there's something about people getting engaged that always makes you think about yourself. I realized that I had avoided Hayden long enough, and that he deserved to know the truth.

"So what are you going to do?" she asked.

I straightened up on the couch and smoothed out my hair. "First, I am going to take a shower. Then I am going to call Hayden and tell him what happened with Michael."

"I think that's for the best," she said sympathetically. "But honestly, do you have feelings for Michael?"

"I do," I said without hesitation. "I have feelings for them both."

"Well, decide quickly so you know who to bring as your date to my engagement party," she said. "Except Michael will probably already be invited because he's going to be one of Alex's groomsmen."

I allowed myself to laugh. "You already booked a venue for an engagement party?"

"Something small," she said. "At a restaurant in Cobble Hill. I'm sending out the invitations this week. It's on January 29th."

"Right before school starts back up," I said. "One last hurrah."

"I know," she nodded. "I wanted to make sure I got to have one before school got in the way."

"I don't blame you," I grimaced. "Hey, did you hear from the professor? Are you definitely in the work-study program with me?"

"I just heard from him this morning," she said. "And it looks like you and I are going to be spending a lot of time together next semester."

"Thank God!" I threw myself backwards on the couch. "I don't think I could last the entire semester with that man without at least one friendly face there." I sat back up in the couch and looked at Olivia. "Everything is going so well for you, Olivia. You're kind of my role model."

"I wouldn't go that far," she laughed.

"Okay, fair enough."

"Alright, my dear," she stood up, still glowing. "Go take a shower and confess your sins. Call me later and let me know what happens, okay?"

"I will," I muttered. "Tell Alex I said congrats."

"Thank you," she said as she walked out the door.

I sat on the couch for a few more minutes, collecting my thoughts. Here was Olivia. So mature, getting married for crying out loud, and here was I. A complete and total mess. My guilt ate at me more and more as each moment passed. I decided my shower would have to wait a little longer. I reached for my cell phone and called Hayden. He picked up on the first ring.

"Hey, baby!" he said in a downright jocular tone. "How are you feeling? Still sick?"

"I'm not feeling that great," I stammered. "But it's not because I'm sick."

"What do you mean?" he asked, worry in his voice. "What's wrong?"

I paused for a moment. I took a deep breath and commanded myself to be honest with him. He deserved the truth.

"Hayden," I began. "There's something I have to tell you."

"Okay," he said in a near-whisper. "What is it?"

I paused for a moment, pushing back the tears and feelings of shame. Hayden deserved to hear this. There was no turning back now.

"I had sex with someone."

There was a long pause on the other end of the line, followed by the sound of Hayden inhaling sharply.

"Who was it?" he asked, anger in his voice.

I swallowed hard. I was suddenly petrified, I had never heard Hayden's voice sound this way before. I thought about lying, telling him it was someone he didn't know. Telling him it was a one-time thing, and that it didn't matter to me. But then I realized, I had to stop lying. To everyone.

"I am so sorry," I began what would be a long string of apologies. "It was Michael."

Chapter 32

Olivia

"You're engaged!" my dad practically shouted into the phone. "That's so wonderful!"

I had been pacing back and forth around my apartment, worried about how my parents would react to the news. My first call was to my dad. I figured he would be supportive; he was good like that. But I knew the next call would have to be to my mother. She wasn't exactly what I would call a supportive figure in my life.

After my parents divorced, I was old enough to decide who I wanted to live with. I chose my father because we had always gotten along so much better than my mom and me. I don't think my mom ever really forgave me for that. I don't think she really understood why I made that decision.

"Thanks, Dad," I said. "I'm scared to call Mom."

"Oh right," he said, his voice suddenly dropping an octave. "That woman can be kind of frightening. Why do you think we got divorced so many years ago?"

I laughed. "Good point. Well I am sending out invitations to my engagement dinner on January 29th. It's going to be here in Brooklyn. Think you can make it in from Rhode Island?"

"Honey," he started. "Wild horses couldn't keep me away. Besides, I think it's about time I met the young man who's going to become my son-in-law."

I floated around the apartment and pushed back the curtains in my bedroom to get a better look out the window. It was snowing again. I felt a flush of warmth as I immediately remembered the snow on New Year's Eve.

"Sorry I haven't been home in a while, Dad," I said, watching the snow fall. "I really miss you."

"I understand. School comes first. But I will see you soon!"

I hung up with my dad and spun around my bedroom. He was undoubtedly calling everyone he knew, telling them I was engaged. This just made it all the more official. After I called my mother and endured her belittling, the whole world would know.

I thought about not calling her. Maybe it would be better for everyone if she just heard from one of my aunts. Or read my engagement announcement in a local paper. I reached for my cell and shot Alex a quick text.

About to call my mom, ugh. Wish me luck!

A moment later my phone buzzed with a return message.

Good luck, babe!

I jumped up and down with nerves and then looked at my engagement ring to calm me down. I smiled when I thought about becoming Alex's wife. I loved him so much, I wasn't going to let her ruin this for me.

I sat at my small bistro table, with a cup of tea and slowly dialed her number. As the phone rang, I said a silent prayer that it would go to voicemail.

She picked up on the third ring.

"Hello?" she asked, as if she didn't have caller ID.

"Hi, Mom, it's Olivia. I have some important news to tell you."

I heard her smoking in the background. "Oh yeah? What is it?"

I reached for my own cigarettes and lit one up. I really needed it while talking to my mother.

"Well," I said through a shaky voice. "I'm getting married."

Silence.

"Mom?" I took a drag of my cigarette. "Are you there?"

Chapter 33

Amalia

The restaurant Olivia chose to have her engagement party at could be described as urban-chic. There were walls of exposed reddish-brown brick, yet the table was set with expensive china. The doors were made of a heavy, thick wood, which gave the restaurant a warm and rustic feeling. But as I glanced at the wine list, I noticed a bottle of Cabernet I had recently brought at Trader Joe's marked up for nearly triple the price. If this restaurant wasn't the quintessence of up-and-coming Brooklyn, then nothing was.

"Hi Mister Davis!" I said, as Olivia's father approached me. I pulled him in for a hug. "Congratulations!"

"Thank you, Amalia." He said through a wide grin. "You look lovely this evening."

"Thank you," I smiled, although I felt awful. After I called Hayden and told him the entire truth, he asked me the exact same question Olivia did. What did I want to do? Who did I want to be with? Him or Michael?

I sauntered around the restaurant lost in my thoughts until I saw a familiar face that stopped me dead in my tracks. What was Cassandra doing here? She was standing by herself with what appeared to be a Martini in her hand. She looked utterly bored. I slowly made my way over to her.

"Hey" I said, trying to hide the shock in my voice. "I didn't expect to see you here."

She pursed her lips together. "Olivia invited me. It felt rude to not attend."

"Right," I muttered. Obviously her only reason for showing face was out of some ridiculous idealized social etiquette, and not to congratulate her friend. "So how've you been?"

"Great," she gave me a phony smile and started looking around the room. "You?"

I shook my head and narrowed my eyes a bit. "You know, Cassandra, not so great."

Shifting her weight between her high heels, she raised an eyebrow at me. She was wearing a little black dress, a bright-pink statement necklace, small stud earrings, and her blonde hair hung pin- straight down to her shoulders. Cassandra didn't address my comment. She merely kept the fake smile plastered on her face and sipped her gin Martini.

I couldn't take it anymore. The refinement tug-of-war was getting to be too much for me. "Seriously, Cassie. What the hell is going on with you?"

She looked taken aback, obviously not expecting me to be so direct with her. "What are you talking about?"

I caught Olivia out of the corner of my eye. She was dragging Alex around, showing him off to everyone like a prize she had won at a county fair. He didn't seem to mind, though.

"I'm talking about your general attitude towards me and pretty much everything around you lately," I blurted out.

"I don't know what you're talking about," she remained composed and ran her hands over her already-smooth hair.

"Oh really?" I asked, not so composed. "How was Christmas Eve this year? Did you and your family have a nice time?"

"It was fine," she said, avoiding eye contact.

I shook my head. I probably looked a little crazy, but I honestly didn't care. "Fine? That's all I get? I came to your parent's house

217

every year for Christmas since we were kids and this year you don't so much as extend me an invitation, and now all you have to say to me is that it was fine?"

"You could have called me too," she snapped.

This comment sent me well over the edge.

"I *have* been calling you, Cass," venom secreting out of my voice. "I have been calling, texting, sending up fucking smoke signals, doing anything and everything that I can do get you to hang out with me. But every time I call you, you don't pick up. If I try to leave you a voice message, your mailbox is always full. Every time I text you, you don't answer. So excuse me if I didn't think it was appropriate for me to just show up at your parents' house on Christmas Eve with a fucking Candy-Gram like it was business as usual after not hearing from you for nearly two months."

Cassandra's eyes began to dart around the room. She kept shaking her head and taking small sips of her drink to give her something to do with her hands.

"I've called you," she scoffed.

"Oh really?" I laughed. "I guess my battery just must have been dead every time you tried to ring me over the past six months. Because last time I checked, I hadn't received a phone call from you since before I left for Brazil."

I knew I was being loud, but I didn't care. I caught Olivia's eye, worried she would give me a dirty look, but instead she gave me a nod. That's when I realized she invited Cassandra here deliberately, so we could have it out. I nodded back to her and shrugged. Thanks, Olivia.

"This is a party, Amalia," Cassie declared as if she was schooling me on my social graces. "It isn't the place to have this conversation." Cassandra put down her drink and reached for her coat. "If you want to talk about this another time when you're more calm, give me a call."

I crossed in front of her. "Why? So you can dodge me some more? No, Cassandra, this is it. No more calling. No more texting.

218

No more avoiding. You either talk to me about this right now, or not at all. I am not going to spend the next few months pathetically trying to drag details of your life out of you when you so obviously couldn't care any less about mine. You either apologize for not inviting me over for Christmas, or for barely being my friend for the past few months *right* now, or I am not speaking to you anymore." I took a step back from her and looked her up and down. "I am so tired of our conversations revolving around your damn schedule."

She shook her head and opened her mouth to say something, but apparently changed her mind. The next thing I knew she was storming out of the restaurant. The door slammed behind her, and everyone turned to look.

"So what happened?" Olivia asked, rushing to my side.

"This is your special day," I said, anger rising in my chest. "Please, don't even worry about it."

"Just tell me. Did the two of you work it out?"

"What do you think?" I cocked my head to the side.

"She's a bitch."

I nodded.

I was so done with worrying about whether or not Cassandra was going to show up places or be up for having a normal conversation with her. If she wanted us to be friends again, she'd have to put the effort in this time. As far as I was concerned, I was done.

"I couldn't help but notice that Hayden's not with you today," Olivia said in a sympathetic voice.

"We're taking some time," I answered softly. It was hard. Hayden and I hadn't even seen each other since before he left for his trip. After our phone call he said we should both take some time to think about what we want. Hearing the pain in Hayden's voice had made me feel like a horrible person. But I deserved to feel badly. I had hurt him. "We're going to talk more about us tomorrow. I need to come to some sort of decision soon."

"I'm here if you need me," she touched my shoulder.

Olivia went back to join Alex, her father, and a woman with short brown hair who I assumed was her mother. I found my place card and decided to sit down at the table. When I got there, sure enough, Michael was already planted in the seat next to mine.

I sat down and tried to avoid eye contact. He had texted me once since our encounter, but I never wrote him back. I honestly had no idea what to say. I couldn't even think straight when it came to him and Hayden.

What was it with me and parties? Each one seemed to be worse than the last.

"Hey," he said, offering me a weak smile.

"Hi," was all I could muster up.

I looked over at him. He was wearing a light-gray button-down shirt with a coordinating darker gray V-neck sweater pulled over it. I looked down at my own outfit. A short red cocktail dress, black cardigan, with black ballet flats. There was no use in me even trying to pull off heels with the amount of ice on the ground outside.

"So," he stirred his drink. "School starts back up on Monday."

I was still reeling from my conversation with Cassandra. I slowly turned my head to face him and give him the brunt of my anger. I know we hadn't spoken, and that mainly it was my fault, but to talk to me about school as if what happened between us meant nothing? I couldn't keep quiet.

"That's all you have to say to me? We hook up, I may have possibly ruined any shot I had with having a real relationship with Hayden, and you and I haven't even spoken since and all you have to say to me is some comment about school?"

Michael said nothing. He just looked down at his drink.

"Of course," I mumbled, crossing my legs and shifting away from him.

"I'm sorry," he said.

"I bet."

"Okay, you know what? I'm not sorry," he leaned in towards me.

"What?" I said, my eyes wide with anxiety.

"I'm not sorry we slept together," he said. "I've been wanting to do that since you got back."

I shook my head. "You were dating Angela."

"Barely," he scoffed. "The whole time I was thinking about you."

"Give me a break, Michael," I said in a defeated tone.

"What do you want from me?" he asked quietly.

More guests were beginning to arrive, stacking presents for Olivia and Alex on a table in the middle of the room. Olivia's life seemed so normal. I knew right then and there I wanted to have a life like that.

"I think the more pertinent question here is what do *you* want from *me*?" I uttered.

He pulled my chair closer to his. "Amalia, would you please just look at me?"

"Fine," I said, in a childish tone. "I'm looking at you. Are you happy now?"

"Could you just drop the defensive attitude for two seconds?"

"I asked you a question," I said in a calmer voice to appease him. "What do you want from me?"

"I want the same thing I wanted back in May," he said in an unwavering tone. "I want what I talked to you about before you left for Brazil. I want to date you."

"Right," I mumbled. "You want to date me, but you don't want to be in a relationship with me."

"Not right away," he said, softening for just a moment. "But how is that any different from you and Hayden? I'm sorry, maybe it's none of my business but the two of you have been together since September and you're still not an official couple."

He had me there. Touché, Michael.

"That, right there, makes me think that you don't want to rush into anything either," he continued.

I didn't say anything. I just sat there for a moment, studying Michael's face.

"So the way I see it here, you have a choice to make," he said declaratively, putting his hands in the steeple position like he was giving an inaugural address.

I threw my hands in the air. "What are you talking about?"

He leaned in closer and repeated himself. "You have a choice, Amalia. You can either choose to keep dating Hayden, which I am thinking you probably will. Or you can step out of your comfort zone, take a chance, and date me."

"Date you?" I said. "With no possibility of it turning into a real relationship."

"That's not what I said," he uttered. "I said I wanted to take it slow."

"I have to think about this," I looked down at the table.

"I would be surprised if you didn't," he said, plucking his napkin off his lap and lightly tossing it on the table. "But please, Amalia, I don't want to wait around forever." He stood up and smoothed out a wrinkle on his sweater. "I'm going to give you until the end of February to decide."

I just looked at him. Was he really saying this to me?

Before I could answer, he gave me a subtle nod and walked away. Stunned, I reached for the pitcher of water on the table and poured myself a generous amount. I rubbed my head and for a moment, it felt like the room was spinning.

I was almost positive I was having an anxiety attack.

Olivia must have noticed my disoriented state because the next thing I knew, she was dragging me outside for some fresh air.

'It's freezing out here!" I nearly shouted as soon as she got me outside.

"You look like you're going to throw up," she said in a mothering tone. "How much have you had to drink?"

"Nothing! Michael just came over to talk to me."

"How did that go?" she asked, sounding slightly annoyed.

I decided to tell her the truth. "Well, Olivia, it appears I have been given ultimatums by not one, but two men in my life."

"What do you mean?"

I pulled my jacket around me tighter and made a silent vow that one day I would move somewhere much warmer.

"Michael came up to me and told me he wants to date me. He gave me a speech not unlike the one he gave me last year. The thing is, he told me I have only until the end of February to decide."

"Wow," she said in a breathy laugh. "That's a large pill to swallow. Now, what's the other ultimatum?"

"After I told Hayden what happened with Michael, he was understandably pretty upset. He told me if I wanted us to stay together then I essentially needed to cut the crap and make it official with him. We would need to be dating exclusively, and I would have to promise that nothing like what happened with Michael would ever happen again."

"That sounds fair," Olivia said. "The two of you have been dating for nearly six months."

"There's one more thing," I said. "Hayden also told me that if he and I stay together, I have to cut Michael out of my life entirely."

Olivia just nodded.

"Don't you think that's a bit extreme?" I asked with wide eyes. I already knew the answer, but I was still looking to be let off the hook for what I did.

"No, I don't," she answered quickly. "You had sex with him, Amalia." She shook her head and I felt her being a little judgmental. "I know it's going to be hard, considering you have to see him at school, but how do you think you would feel if the situation was reversed? I'm sorry, but I understand where Hayden's coming from."

My shoulders sank and I let out a sigh. "I guess I do too." I started to shiver from the harsh winter wind.

"I'm not trying to make you feel bad, I just want you to know that I don't think Hayden's being unreasonable," she softened.

"You're right," I let out a sigh. "He's not."

"And honestly, are you and Michael going to be pals if you pick Hayden? How long will you be able to grab coffee together,

223

and hang out on the High Line before one of you starts wanting more again?"

She was right. Michael and I had never really been just friends. There had always been underlying tension, even when I was dating Nicholas.

So what are you going to do, Amalia?" She raised both of her eyebrows. "Who are you going to pick?"

There I was, faced with a similar choice to last year's. Only this time, there was another person's feelings to consider. Hayden's. No matter what, I had to come to some sort of decision. There was no running away this time. No flights booked, no packed bags, no escape. Both guys lived in New York and this was a small island.

I had to make a choice.

I looked at Olivia, who was patiently waiting for me to answer.

"You're a good friend, you know that?" I said, allowing myself to smile for the first time in days. "That's why I know I can trust you. I know who I am going to pick. But if I tell you, you have to promise not to tell anyone. Not even Alex."

"I can do that," she nodded.

"Good," I grinned. I looked back and forth and whispered my answer in her ear. I didn't want *anyone* from the party overhearing us.

I stepped back to gauge her reaction. Her face remained neutral.

"I promise," she said, putting her right hand over her heart. "I won't tell anyone."

"We'll talk about it more tomorrow," I said, nervously twirling my hair. "But for right now let's go back inside and enjoy your engagement party!"

"Wait! One more thing," she uttered, just as I turned to go back inside. "I was wondering if you would consider being my maid-of-honor?"

"Hell, yeah!" I nearly shouted. Olivia beamed and lightly tugged on the end of her dress. She did a quick twirl and we both laughed

I held the door open for her and we walked back into the

restaurant together. As soon as I got inside, my phone began to buzz. It was a message from Hayden. A moment later Michael caught my eye and smiled. I put my phone back in my purse and went to introduce myself to Olivia's mother.

I knew who I was going to choose. But for right now, I wasn't going to think about that. Tonight, I had one job. I was going to assume the position of Olivia's maid-of-honor. Tonight was about my fabulous friend and her wonderful news. So I raised a glass of champagne to toast Olivia and her new husband-to-be.

Everything else could wait for another day.